W9-CKJ-582

A   Dewhurst, Eileen

There was a Little Girl

DATE DUE
$6.50

FEB 13 '86	MAR 3 '87	
	JUL 5 1988	
FEB 22 '89		
MAR 13 1986	14 '88	
APR 8 1900	JUL	
APR 26 1986	SEP 24 '88	
MAY 8 1986		
JUL 3 1986		
NOV 29 1986 SEP 9		
FEB 7		

HOPE WELTY TWP. LIBRARY
Box 368 · 116 E. Wait
Cerro Gordo, Ill. 61818

HOPE WELTY TWP. LIBRARY
Box 368 · 116 E. Wait
Cerro Gordo, Ill. 61818

THERE WAS
A LITTLE GIRL

Jan 1986 - St'cLay - $6.50

By Eileen Dewhurst
THERE WAS A LITTLE GIRL
THE HOUSE THAT JACK BUILT
WHOEVER I AM
CURTAIN FALL
TRIO IN THREE FLATS
DRINK THIS
AFTER THE BALL
DEATH CAME SMILING

THERE WAS
A LITTLE GIRL

EILEEN DEWHURST

PUBLISHED FOR THE CRIME CLUB BY
DOUBLEDAY & COMPANY, INC.
GARDEN CITY, NEW YORK
1986

All the characters in this book
are fictitious, and any resemblance
to actual persons, living or dead,
is purely coincidental.

Library of Congress Cataloging in Publication Data
Dewhurst, Eileen.
    There was a little girl.
    I. Title.
PR6054.E95T5   1986   823'.914
ISBN 0-385-23230-6

LIBRARY OF CONGRESS CATALOG CARD NUMBER 85–13177
COPYRIGHT © 1984 BY EILEEN DEWHURST
ALL RIGHTS RESERVED
PRINTED IN THE UNITED STATES OF AMERICA
FIRST EDITION IN THE UNITED STATES OF AMERICA

To Phyl Mellor

THERE WAS
A LITTLE GIRL

CHAPTER 1

In the month since Bertha had last made this early-morning journey, the landscape at seven had gained dramatically in light. At the end of January there had been no indication in the sky that day was at hand, and the lamps in the village street had still glowed brightly against blackness. Now, with February almost gone, even though it was colder and there was a frost, the sun was already appearing out of the orange flush which seemed to rise from the ground behind the bare trees edging the heath. When she came for Juliet at the end of March, it would be full day . . .

The entrance to Bellfield House was so generous she didn't have to take care as she drove between the lion-crowned gateposts. Juliet was on the steps, a small picture in the elaborate frame of the Victorian-renaissance portico, neatly dressed in her navy blue school coat. Her blue bag hung over her shoulder, and the usual small suitcase was at her feet. As she saw the car, Juliet picked up the suitcase and ran down the steps. Bertha leaned across to unlock the passenger door.

"Hop in, Miss Earlybird."

"I think it's a bit late, Auntie."

Juliet responded to the presentation of her aunt's cheek as she always did, with a swift gesture that scarcely made contact. Bertha sighed, released the brake. "I don't think I'm late." Juliet was composing herself and her belongings in her seat, not turning her head again. "You'd hate to miss these weekends of yours, wouldn't you?"

"I like going to London." The quiet voice hadn't answered immediately. "Can you meet me tomorrow?"

"Of course, dear."

The tree-shaded lane, still almost dark, yielded in the marvellously abrupt way of the New Forest to a stretch of heath. The sky was all at once so bright Bertha lowered the shield onto the wind-screen. A mist hovered low over the heather, and the brown and grey backs of the scattered ponies seemed to be floating in space.

"I haven't heard you play for a long time. Is Mr. Marian still pleased with you?"

Bertha was aware of the rise and fall of Juliet's shoulders.

"He doesn't praise, Auntie. He gets frustrated, I think, that he only sees me once a month. I wish I could go up once a fort-night."

"Daddy said that perhaps you can next year, if you do well in the exam. I think that's fair, don't you?"

"Fair? Oh yes, I suppose so."

"Will you come back to supper with me tomorrow when I've collected you from Brockenhurst?"

"Yes, of course, if you'll tell them at the house. Thank you."

"Good." Sometimes it made her feel almost foolish, to be so much more enthusiastic, at her age, than someone young. "Anything special you'd like to eat? I expect you'll have a good lunch at the flat."

"I expect so. I'll just have whatever you're having, Auntie."

"Right you are."

Bertha sighed once more and turned her spare attention to the contrasts of earth and sky. Neither aunt nor niece spoke again until Bertha drew up outside Brockenhurst station.

Always, these early mornings, she arrived and departed with the minimum of delay, never switching off the engine. But today, as Juliet was pressing the catch of the door, Bertha spoke her name without first saying good-bye, and the girl was suddenly stock-still.

"Are you all right, dear?" continued Bertha.

The pale, slightly freckled face, as neat and shapely as the clothes and the dark hair, and as expressionless, turned slowly back to her.

"Of course, Auntie. Why ever should you think I'm not?"

But there was no question in the wide green eyes.

"I don't know really, dear. I've just felt . . . For some time, really . . ."

"What, Auntie?"

Juliet's hand was gripping her bag strap unnecessarily tight. Her knuckles showed white.

"Oh, just that perhaps you weren't . . . as happy as you used to be."

Juliet's laugh, too, failed to reach her eyes.

"You're imagining things, Auntie. It's just that I'm working hard, I've got O-levels in June."

"Yes, of course. I've been meaning to mention, by the way, dear —don't you think it's time we thanked Mrs. Hardman for having you to stay so regularly?"

The blue strap jerked on Juliet's shoulder. "There's no need. She knows Carol can come and stay with us at Bellfield House any time, and I just fit in with whatever they're doing. I'll have to go now, Auntie, I'll miss the train. I'll ring you when I get to the flat tonight."

"Bless you, I know you will. Off you go."

Juliet got quickly out of the car, and through the mirror Bertha saw her niece vanish into the station building as, sighing yet again, she drove away.

The sun now was radiantly golden, and already the frosty pallor was fading from grass and hedge. Among the heather the beasts were once more anchored to earth by strong slender legs. But Bertha, busy with her thoughts, no longer saw them . . .

It *was* some time since she'd first thought Juliet was growing quiet, elusive. She'd been going to mention it to Leonard the night he had had his heart attack and died, and Leonard had been dead three years. Juliet had been twelve then. Perhaps the onset of puberty . . .

In the elegant hall of Bellfield House, Bertha encountered her brother.

"Good morning, Henry."

The anxious face brightened.

"Bertha! You've come for Juliet? It really is so awfully good—"

"I came for her half an hour ago. I'm just back from dropping her at the station. Really, Henry. But I suppose it's something that you remembered it was her music weekend."

"I'm sorry, dear. The new course, it's rather exercising me and I'm—"

"D'you think Juliet's all right?"

"What's that?"

The tall, untidy figure had turned away and was trying to examine one of many lists pinned to a notice board.

"Henry! I asked you, do you think Juliet's all right?"

"All right? Juliet? Why shouldn't she be?"

"No reason, that's why I'm asking you. I know you're principal of Bellfield College and an authority on Roman architecture, but you are also a father. Of a motherless girl."

"All right, Bertha." With visible effort her brother anchored himself in the moment. "What's up with Juliet?"

The sister now looked the more uncertain of the two.

"I don't know. Nothing, perhaps. Or perhaps just growing up. I thought you might have sensed something."

The principal rubbed the top of his head, leaving a thin tuft of hair upright on the crown. "Oh dear. I can't say I have. You're quite right, Bertha, I don't pay as much attention to Juliet as I ought to. I'll try . . ." Suddenly the soft, slow voice was almost eager. "I heard her practising last night. It sounded awfully good."

Bertha patted his arm. "I'm sure it did. And I'm sure really there's nothing to worry about. Now, I'll get along to the office and try to deal with anyone or anything which doesn't want to wait until Monday. And some of the flowers must need renewing."

Closing the office door behind her, Bertha sat down, picked up the telephone receiver and dialled. The call was answered almost at once.

"John? Hello, dear, cheap rate Saturday, it's your stepmama." She spoke the title as if it was inside inverted commas. "Remember? Bertha, second wife of your deceased papa . . . *That*'s right." She was playing with the short gold chain round her throat. "I've just got back from taking Juliet to her train and I had an idea . . . *Juliet*. My brother Henry's daughter . . . *That*'s it. She goes to this marvellous musical Pole for piano lessons once a month. She's at his place all day Saturday, then spends Saturday night and Sunday morning—wasn't there a film called that?—with her friend Carol Hardman and Carol's parents.

They've a flat in Knightsbridge . . . As you say, not bad . . . John, why don't you take Juliet out to lunch on Sunday, it would just fit in nicely before her train home? You and she always got on so well, she'd be thrilled . . . No, of course you can't, just like that, I wasn't necessarily meaning this month. Anyway, the Hardmans will have catered for her tomorrow. She leads such a quiet life at the college. In Bellfield. It would do her good, encourage her to talk . . . It's awful, but I can't remember the Hardman number offhand and I'm sure Henry won't know it. I hardly ever use it, anyway, Juliet always rings me after her lesson. On Saturday evening, never misses. It'll be under Hardman in the book . . . Hardman . . . Knightsbridge, as I said. You're so *near* . . . How are you, by the way? . . . Oh, I'm all right . . ." Bertha turned her head and looked appraisingly at her face in the mirror on the wall beside the desk. Then back towards the window, where the highly cultivated garden faded into the heath —the forest donkey was more noticeable than the old wall on which its head was resting. "John, do think about taking Juliet out for lunch. All work and no play's making Jill—well, not a dull girl, but a rather too serious one, I think. By the way, I may be coming up to town in a week or two, any chance of lunch for *me?* . . . Of course it depends, I realize that, I'd give you notice . . . All right, off you go . . . 'Bye . . . Come in!"

The office door opened as Bertha replaced the receiver, and a young man edged into the room. Slight and fair, he had pink cheeks of a bloom more usually associated with childhood, and large worried blue eyes.

"Good morning, Peter. I don't suppose I can do for you what Miss Booth would do, but—"

The pink flooded scarlet. "Oh, that's all right, Mrs. Hazell, I wasn't expecting . . ." It was clear the young man had been expecting an empty office. "I only wanted to look at a list. My course on Keats is on Monday and I just wanted to see . . . It's all right, I know where it'll be . . ."

With a self-deprecating smile, he approached a drawer whose opening was contingent upon Bertha removing her elbow from the desk. She sat watching him as he rummaged, amused in a sympathetic way by his embarrassment even though she was getting used to it, reflecting that he had been Bellfield's resident lecturer in English long enough to become attracted by Juliet, but not long enough to approach his reponsibilities without trepidation. But it was his first post after university, and she was inclined to be tolerant.

"I suppose you've been taking Juliet to the station, Mrs. Hazell. It's her London Saturday, isn't it?"

Peter's head was bent over the open drawer.

"That's right." On the whole, Bertha approved of such evidence that the young man's devotion to his new duties was not entirely single-minded. Not that Juliet was old enough for a boyfriend, although these days girls and boys started going out together so very young, and not only that . . .

At this point Bertha always switched her thoughts with a shudder, but Juliet did lead rather a cloistered life, it would do her good to have lunch with John, and a male friend on the spot might not be a bad thing, especially one so essentially harmless and so well educated as Peter Cowley . . .

With a pang, Bertha found herself wishing that Peter Cowley was her son, an idea too painful to entertain now the physical option was no longer open. Certainly he would make a more satisfactory stepson than John . . .

Slitting open the post when Peter had left the office still murmuring apologies, Bertha realized how much she liked Saturday mornings. They were the one time of the week when she had a clearly defined role at Bellfield House, when Henry and his staff were glad to have her sitting in the office sorting the letters and answering the telephone, because Miss Booth only came in Mondays to Fridays. And it would soon be her twice-yearly Bellfield course, An Introduction to English Furniture, which she always so much enjoyed—it was so satisfactory to be able to sit with one's students in the bar between sessions, and eat among them at mealtimes, all without any more travel than the few minutes' walk or drive from home. But she enjoyed her WEA classes too, and the one-off invitations to luncheon and supper clubs. These later stages of her life would really be very good, if only what she wanted most in the world could happen, or she cease to care whether or not it did.

CHAPTER 2

Cathy led the way for the third or fourth time across the public landing.

"I know it's silly, Neil, but I always think the small, unimportant decisions are the hardest to make. I mean, when someone faces me with a very large menu I can never . . . But I'm quite enjoying this, aren't you?"

Her radiant smile embraced him from head to toe.

"I know it's silly, but I am."

"As soon as I get into one flat, I sort of can't weigh up the other." Cathy looked back from the open doorway of Neil's flat towards the open doorway of her own. "But I like the shape of your kitchen better, even though I do get more sun."

"You certainly get more sun." Neil turned away from his sitting room, from his awareness of its exclusive association with himself and his lifelong relish of independence, and put his hands on Cathy's shoulders. "That's very important, almost as important as the thing which clinches it."

"So you've decided." He could tell she was trying to look indifferent, probably trying to feel indifferent, and in his grateful affection he kissed the tip of her nose.

"Yes. Of course we've got to live in your flat. You've signed it. How could we abandon your signature? All those one-day-to-be-priceless murals?"

"But you've said . . . a house . . ." Her pleasure was showing through.

"That's different. When we move to a house, it'll be out of sight, out of mind. That is, if there isn't already a blue plaque on Westcote Gardens. While we're still here . . . Think how we'd feel if we saw men in white overalls with paint-stained ladders being let into your old flat. Anyway, our homelife so far has been with you." He realized this as he said it. That Cathy's flat had always been open to him, as never his to her. "Yes. *Yes.* I'll see Rigby in the morning about putting this on the market, and I'll arrange for my few good pieces to go into store. The desk and the chest of drawers . . . It won't be for all that long."

"I don't mind how long we stay here."

"You will. We must have a garden. And a cat. And could we have some coffee? At your place?"

"Of course!"

The corn-coloured bloom of her hair briefly illumined the outside landing. About to follow her, Neil turned back into his own flat and made a quick valedictory tour. It was as if he had to inform the place right away of what was to happen. Not that he cared all that much; it was only that giving it up was a symbol of the enormous change in his life that marriage would bring.

"Marriage to Cathy."

He said the words aloud, standing in the middle of his sitting room. As always, they warmed and reassured him, reaffirmed the gulf between the concepts of marrying (which was as unthinkable as it had always been) and marrying this particular woman (which was inevitable). And to have to say the words at all, that was only a carryover of old reflexes which every day were slower . . .

"Marriage to Cathy."

He had had to say the words the night before, in his soul, in that smoky, strobe-lit bar, in order to get up and say good night and leave. It had troubled him a bit all day, vaguely, that he had needed to say them, that as yet his instinct wasn't strong enough for him always to do the things he now preferred to do without the defilement of reluctance . . . No, it hadn't been reluctance, he had wanted to get up and leave, leave that bright, sharp little face bending towards him with teasing eyes, it was only that he had found himself, until he said those three words, going on sitting there, responding, leaning forward in his turn, in the way he had done heedlessly for all his adult life. He and his sergeant had gone into the bar on a tip-off, they'd started talking to the two young girls in the way of police business, buying them a drink apiece, chatting them up, going through the sort of routine getting married wasn't going to alter, couldn't alter if he went on being a good copper. But even when they had discovered the girls weren't the pair they were after, he'd gone on being aware of this one, of the way she crossed her legs, her thigh, feeling the old connections with all the times in the past, even telling her his name and his rank . . .

"Marriage to Cathy."

What was he worrying about? He hadn't done anything wrong, he hadn't wanted to do anything wrong, he had got up and told his sergeant to come along; it was just that he suddenly wanted his thoughts and words to match his deeds . . . And perhaps the girl—Marilyn, she had told him she was called—had reminded him of Cathy because, behind her makeup and her knowingness, she had Cathy's deceptive aura of extreme youth.

Cathy. All at once he couldn't wait to see her again, banging his front door and running across to hers, which awaited him open. Awaited him and nobody else. His luck was incredible.

She didn't question his fierce embrace, merely asking him, after one equal returning pressure, if he would like a biscuit.

"Why not?" He took the tray from her and followed her dancing steps into her sitting room. He set the tray down. "Isn't it time you booked the church?"

"Neil!" Cathy precipitated herself onto him, but drew back before things got difficult. Neil had said only once how he intended to try and conduct the engagement, but he thought she always tried to make it as easy for him as possible. How difficult it was for her he didn't yet know . . .

With an effort, he turned away from the dazzling prospect.

"All right, all right. Why so much excitement?"

"Because I wasn't really sure you wanted the church. I know you never go, and—"

"I was brought up to go."

"So were lots of people. Neil, I wouldn't want you to feel you were taking part in— in something that didn't seem real to you." She could have no idea how troubled her face was.

"I don't disbelieve. I shall be quite happy to be married in your village church."

He couldn't bring himself to tell her he would in fact be happier in the church than in the register office, perhaps because he didn't know, or want to examine, the reason.

"Dearest Neil, thank you. I don't go every Sunday, as you very well know, but I feel I should when I don't." The troubled look edged back. "I wish we could do without most of Mummy's and Daddy's friends and all the dressing up. But it won't be so bad with only little tiny bridesmaids."

"Cathy!" He made a quick caricature of her bear hug. "That's marvellous! It cuts out Winnie." The only way not to have Winnie, Cathy's impossible friend from home whom she had outgrown but to whom she remained loyal, was not to have any adult bridesmaids. Cathy was doing it for him, but Neil thought she might be suiting her own inclinations as well.

"Poor Winnie," said Cathy severely. "Nobody ever seems to love her."

"Except you. It's her own fault for being so supremely unlovable. She'd start neighing in the very aisle, I know she would. And even in the congregation . . . She won't be away next month by any chance?"

"No! Neil, I think I'll go home this weekend. Give Mummy the glad news that she can make me a full-scale wedding dress. Rally the small cousins."

"May I come with you?"

"Of course." She put out her hand to him, and the only alternative as he took it was to pull her to her feet, then let it go. As further distraction he asked her if she really was happy with the prospect of a week in small old West Country hotels.

"You know I am. It was one of the ways I saw—you and me—when it seemed—impossible. Arriving on a chilly evening to a fire in the hall, then going upstairs to the same room and bed."

She looked at him apologetically, as if she thought she had been unfair, but he hid his intense reaction.

"It'll still be chilly in April. We'll go abroad for a week in the summer during your school holidays. I promise."

"I don't mind."

"I know you don't. I'm going now."

To the old world across the landing.

"Good night, Neil darling. It's not quite four weeks."

She smiled at him, adding one more to his many moments of struggle not to live down to his old reputation.

Four weeks was a lifetime.

And it did seem to pass with unique slowness, a long-drawn-out end to the first phase of his life. A dreamlike time, perhaps because, with his working days being as they had always been, his marriage and its aftermath seemed at moments to be something so unlikely he must awaken and find them lost. He worked each evening as late as he could, hoping to weaken his nightly temptation through tiredness as much as by willpower, and on Friday nights or Saturday mornings drove down to Cathy's parents' with a sense of deliverance.

Except for the ultimate weekend, when she had final fittings and might anyway like to be at home for the last time as Cathy McVeigh. He saw her off in her little car with a mingling of relief and anxiety. He could smile at his anxiety—he had seen her drive away alone, in the years they had been no more than neighbours, time after time without a qualm—but he couldn't dispel it. He was glad he had volunteered for full weekend duty.

The telephone call came mid-Sunday morning. His sergeant answered it and shouted across to him, his hand over the mouthpiece. "For you, governor. Female. Are you here?"

"For heaven's sake!"

He'd spoken to Cathy before leaving his flat, but she was the only female, and the ridiculous solicitude leapt in him again. He tried not to run across the room.

"Yes? Yes?"

"Detective Inspector Neil Carter?"

He thought for an absurd moment that Cathy was teasing him, and the voice was not unlike her voice.

"It is."

"Is it? Really?"

He sensed the pleased surprise.

"Yes. Who is that?"

"Marilyn. It's Marilyn. You remember Marilyn."

For a moment he didn't, his head full of pictures of the Mc-

Veigh household in some kind of disarray, but reluctantly he recalled the evening he had put out of his mind.

"Marilyn?" He would not so readily admit to his memory.

"Neil! At Adrian's. You bought me nice drinkies. You must remember!"

"I buy quite a few drinks in the course of my duties. However, I think I remember. What can I do for you?"

Why on earth had he uttered his name and his rank? Perhaps it was right he should pay for his indiscretion with discomfort. But nothing more.

"Formal, aren't we?" She would be flouncing, bridling, tossing her head. He tried not to imagine it, to think of her as a pathetic young creature he had been sorry for. But it wouldn't wash. "I'm sure you remember very well. I asked for you because I remember *you* very well. You were nice to me." Beyond the call of duty. Only just. But that was a world too much. "I need protection, Neil. Police protection."

"Why?"

On a reflex he reached for pen and paper, completing the gesture with an almost painful sense of reluctance.

" 'Cos someone's on the way that I'm afraid of. If you don't come now it'll be too late." There was perhaps a hint of hysteria in the exaggerated laughter. He sensed that the vowels in the stage-cockney voice were better formed than the speaker wished.

"If you could tell me a bit more . . . Marilyn."

"I'll tell you when you come. You've got to come, the police have got to come when you ask them."

"If you give me the address, I'll certainly see that someone comes."

"Not someone, Neil. You."

"Or one of my colleagues."

"No. *No.* " There was a pause, in which he thought he heard her yawn. Boredom and apprehension were a strange mixture of emotions, but he could sense both. "You. Please. If you don't come, something terrible could happen."

"What?"

"I can't tell you on the telephone, but I'm dead scared." She paused again, and then the words came quickly. "It makes me sick, the way I can never get away from home, never, never, never." The voice suddenly had been quite different, cold, un-provocative, convincing. A true voice? "Go on, Neil, come and see me, I'll tell you all about it. Neil . . ."

"What's the address?"

Marilyn was restored, her voice again crudely, drawlingly entic-ing. But it was because of that brief other voice that he asked the question.

There was another pause before she told him, as if she was absorbing her second pleasant surprise. "You'll come, then? Now?"

"Now?" His watch said eleven forty-five.

"It has to be now. I shall be in danger any minute."

"I'll come as soon as I can."

"Come now. Or it might be too late. Really."

"Have you a surname?"

There was a trill of laughter, more obviously hysteria-edged. "If I haven't, you won't come?"

"If you want me to help you, you shouldn't obstruct me."

"Oh, Neil, I wouldn't do that, honestly." He thought the appre-hension was growing. "When you come, I'll answer all your ques-tions."

"I hope so."

"I'll leave the key downstairs for you. The porter won't be there till one, as it's Sunday, but I'll leave it in the third pigeonhole behind his desk. C for Carter."

He felt himself stiffen, heard the sudden harshness of his voice. "Why?"

"Because."

"I shall ring your doorbell and you can let me in."

"Maybe I can, maybe I can't. I'll leave the key. Don't pretend not to want to see me, Neil." Dear God, did he really deserve this?

The other receiver went down before he could speak again.

"What's up, governor?"

He thought his face into blandness, in case it was necessary. With amiable, charitable David it probably wasn't. Just looking at

David, blond and usually sunny, made him feel darker, sharper, sallower, more morose than he knew he really was.

"I should have asked you to inquire if it was *my* female. It was one of those two girls we chatted up at Adrian's last month, the wrong two. I said five unnecessary words, and this one remembered them. Marilyn." Somehow he hated simply saying the name. "Said she needs police protection, but wouldn't say why. I'd forget all about it, David, only there was something for a moment in her voice. I'll finish the work on the file we need for Sloane Street, it'll only take ten minutes and then we'll be off. Start with her ladyship and carry straight on."

Now. But he would delay only long enough to prepare the papers for what had been going to be their first outside job and could now be their second without coming back to the office.

He was ready in ten minutes, although it had felt longer because of still hearing that insistent voice in his head. Anyway, Sunday morning, it would be only another ten or fifteen minutes before they arrived, she couldn't expect much better than that.

He elected to drive, he was always exhilarated by Sunday's possibility of unimpeded movement through the streets of central London. The sergeant beside him, he drove behind one other car at a steady thirty the length of Victoria Street, passed the station on his left, crossed Buckingham Palace Road with only one change down, accelerated into the first triangle of Grosvenor Gardens—and braked sharply as the car in front of him screamed to a halt too late to avoid contact with the car trying to beat the lights from Beeston Place.

It was only a glancing blow and no one was hurt, but it had to be sorted out, and by the time the two cars with their respectively apologetic and indignant drivers had gone on their subdued way it was nearly one o'clock.

Only another five or ten minutes, but *now* had taken more than an hour.

It was a Victorian block with curly red roof line, and any one of the flats would probably have paid for Sir Roderick McVeigh's country house. There was no porter behind the mahogany counter, and Neil led the way past, to the lift, ignoring the white envelope he could see sloping across the third of the mahogany pigeonholes.

The lift was as pleasantly old-fashioned as the building, obscuring the view by no more than a stout gilded mesh. As requested, he pressed the button for the second floor and they were clanked slowly aloft. Here, too, there were sofas and palms and thick-piled carpet. The name slot in the front door of flat number twenty-nine was empty. Neil rang the bell.

He heard it ring inside, and again when he pressed it for the second and third times.

"What now, governor?"

"She said she'd leave a key downstairs." He had hoped not to have to tell this to David. "I suppose we'd better get it, and let ourselves in."

He tried to meet David's eye with the innocence anyone but himself would accord himself. They took the lift downstairs again to the entrance hall.

It was a small shock to find a large man in a smart dark green uniform now installed behind the counter.

"I think a key has been left for me." Reluctance seemed to be his sensation of the day. "Detective Inspector Neil Carter." If only he hadn't said it that other time, he wouldn't be saying it now.

The porter also was reluctant.

"Excuse me, sir, but could I ask you to—"

He had his ID close to the porter's florid face, held it there. The man backed slightly to get it in focus.

"Thank you, Inspector Carter, that is satisfactory. There is an envelope here for you."

The man put it into Neil's hand, his expression without curiosity.

"You weren't on duty just now."

If he had expected to disconcert he had failed.

"No, Inspector. Sundays I come on at one o'clock."

Give or take five minutes.

"I see. Thank you." No use asking if the girl had gone out. And even if the porter had been there, he was not disposed to ask him if he had seen Marilyn. It was all absurd, something blowing up out of nothing. Knock three times and ask for Marilyn . . . But he was uneasy.

He opened the envelope in the lift, letting David see the contents. There was nothing but a single Yale key.

He rang the bell again before he used it, waited a few moments afterwards. Then, his reluctance strengthening almost to the point of making him feel queasy, he turned the key in the lock—it moved easily—and pushed open the door.

A hall as big as a room, furnished as a room with mushroom-coloured upholstery and small shining tables.

"In here." He wanted to keep David beside him, and actually put his hand on David's arm as they moved to the doorway from which the light streamed. It was a large drawing room with a long window overlooking the park. He looked enviously round it, hurting the palm of his hand on the key he still clutched.

"Come on." With David there, he couldn't make himself call the name Marilyn, but he hurried across the hall to the next open doorway, and the end of their short search. The girl's body lay across the wide bed.

He thought to himself right away, Marilyn, but it could have been any girl, the body covered over with a white towelling robe, only one upturned palm visible apart from the bare, drooping feet and the distorted face.

"God, Neil."

But his sergeant hadn't been asked to come *now*. If he hadn't stopped to prepare those papers . . .

When he advanced to the bed and peered down, he saw that the stocking—or the tights—was still round the throat. The face was heavily made up, as he remembered it, and the displaced blood scarcely showed through. The eyes stared at the ceiling. He lifted a corner of the robe only enough to see, and to let David see, that the body was naked. Then, aware of the silence, the deep privacy of good building, good carpets and curtains, thanking God that David was there, he put out a hand to the flesh.

It was, as it was bound to be, still warm.

"Governor . . ."

"It's all right, David."

"You're always so tough."

He must make a savage effort. "It's just the thought—if I hadn't stopped to get those papers ready, we wouldn't have met the accident, we'd have got here—"

"Perhaps. Perhaps not. Good Lord, governor, you dropped everything."

"Thanks, David."

Now.

Had he left that moment, when she had asked him, she might still be alive. He had only spoken his name and rank unwisely, and a woman's death was on his hands.

He went slowly back to the hall, David at his heels. This morning, he had been free; now, with a few steps inside a building, he was entangled both with ugly events and with his conscience. Swallowing on his ghastly astonishment, he turned to David.

"There must be another telephone."

"I think in the drawing room."

"If you will, David."

While David was telephoning, Neil looked quickly round the rest of the flat, then forced himself to go back into the bedroom.

There was no sign of struggle, except that the bedside clock was on the floor by the bed with broken glass and the time at twenty-five to one. The bed under the body was disordered, but only in the inevitable way where lovers have wrestled. Staring unhappily at the self-coloured rose of the carpet, he lamented not for the first time the decreasing use of that expensive silky weave on which all foot action and shoe detail leave trace. The room smelt heavy in the familiar way which at this moment made him feel sick. It was an enormous relief that David was appearing in the doorway.

"The team's on its way, governor."

"Thanks, David."

He was afraid his smile must look like a rictus. But that was perhaps to be expected from one who had failed to respond fast enough to a plea which might have prevented the ending of a life. The second cause for disquiet which belonged only to him—his unhappy knowledge that he had earned his involvement, now, through his old frailty a few weeks before—that was something he must from the start practise keeping to himself, since he would speak of it to no one. And no one included Cathy. He had not really been disloyal, and it would be self-indulgent to show her, with this illustration, how exacting his standards had become.

Or at least, this was the way he was going to rationalize it.

"It is that girl, governor?"

"I think it is, yes."

"That handbag would help."

"We'd better wait." The doorbell rang. "I'll take it."

So sure was he it would be the team, even though they had made phenomenally good time, that he could almost see them as he opened the door. But on the step was one young man in jeans and a denim jacket, handsome in a sharp, unsubtle way, brown hair flopping forward on his forehead. His right hand, with something in it, was outstretched towards the door but dropped to his side as he saw Neil. The face, which had been blank, was all at once guarded, suspicious.

"Yes? What do you want?"

"Number twenny-nine, is it? Sorry, wrong door." The vowels were more honestly of London than those the dead girl had spoken.

"Just a minute."

Neil stepped over the threshold and the young man turned and began to walk swiftly towards the lift, accelerating as he went.

"Just a minute!"

Neil and David, at instant full stretch, caught him up as he wheeled past the lift towards the staircase.

"Here! What d'ya mean?"

"We're police officers," said Neil wearily. "And you were going to open the wrong door if somebody inside hadn't opened it for you." David relieved the young man of what he was carrying. "Did you think Marilyn wouldn't be there? Or wouldn't be able to hear the bell?"

The struggle abated and the young man was taken back inside flat number twenty-nine against only verbal protest.

"You've no proof of that. I rang the bell. What's up with Marilyn, anyway?"

"I'll ask the questions. When did you last see her? We can check quite easily, you might as well tell us the truth."

"So I'll tell you the truth. I spent the night with her, so the last time I saw her was this morning."

"Here?"

"Sure. Here."

"What time did you leave?"

The young man and Sergeant Hughes were fitted cosily into the two-seater buttoned settee in the hall which matched the chair opposite, on which Neil was leaning forward. Far enough to smell the sweat which had not been evident when he and David were alone in the flat.

"I left at eight, didn't I?"

"Did you?"

"Yeah, I did. Eight o'bloody clock. I know why."

"You know why—what?" He could see the moisture gleaming on the triangle of forehead which showed beside the flop of hair.

"Why she made me leave early. She was expecting someone. As soon as I arrived, she said she was expecting someone the next morning and I'd have to be on my way sharpish. Madam! I could have given her one for that."

There was something about the boy—appealing was too strong a word—which made Neil think he was probably more talk than action. "Man or woman?"

"She didn't say. But it must have been a man. She's a pro, isn't she?"

"Is she?"

"You tell me."

"That would be rather difficult. So you just left when she asked you? You weren't jealous?"

The man stared. "Jealous? You're joking. But I didn't all that much like being chucked out without my breakfast in bed. All I got was a lousy cup of tea."

"Too bad. Why did you come back just now?"

"Because I left my lighter, didn't I? My gold lighter."

"On one of those little tables in the drawing room," offered David.

"Look, what's all this about? Where's Marilyn? I don't see why I should stand for this."

Nevertheless the young man got to his feet. Neil thought he was annoyed as much by his own lack of aggression as by the situation he found himself in. David was standing beside him, Neil by the front door.

"Take him into one of the other bedrooms, David." The front doorbell rang again. "No, stay here."

The team streamed in. Neil sent them into the main bedroom, detaching one member and directing him and David to a spare bedroom with the young man. When they had let him have the diary from the handbag on the bedroom window ledge, he went into the drawing room, and when he had looked through the diary he rang the chief at home.

"I can't think of any obvious reason why the diary shouldn't belong to the girl. You might like to use the telephone number right away."

"I think I might, Neil. What were you doing in that flat?"

He wondered about the expression on the chief's face as he told him why the girl had been able to ask for him by name. If David hadn't known, Neil would have been tempted to withhold the information. Except that the girl might have written the four words down somewhere. *Detective Inspector Neil Carter.* Then there would have been something out of nothing. Nothing, it was nothing. That was why it was frightening him.

"She rang at a quarter to twelve, governor, and asked me to come right away. We left ten minutes later, when I'd finished preparing the report for what had been going to be our first outside job, and ran into an accident in Grosvenor Gardens which we had to sort out. Got here at one."

"Um. Was she in a panic?"

"I'd say not. She sounded more bored than frightened, but there was something . . ." If he'd cut the conversation off after her first request, they could have been five minutes earlier still.

"You hadn't seen her again, Neil?"

"No, governor."

The chief would have to take his word for it. *Cathy, will you take my word for it?* Cathy, the daughter of such charmingly formidable parents. Their faces filled his mind's eye as he helped David and the young man into the back of the car, drove them to the Yard.

There was a message telling him the chief had come in, and when he presented himself, alone, the chief's face was not as usual, but the difference in his expression was not what Neil had feared.

"Sit down, Neil."

He tried not to let it look like collapse. The chief was certainly not happy, but his eyes were not homing in on his subordinate.

"Governor?" asked Neil at last, into the continuing silence.

The chief heaved himself to his feet, stood glowering at the wall. "Your young pro, Neil, she doesn't come from London. She's a schoolgirl in the New Forest and she's fifteen years old."

CHAPTER 3

Women in floating feminine clothes and wide hats on heads held at slightly awkward angles. Men standing behind them and pulling slyly at unaccustomed short grey waistcoats before coughing into their hands. Small girls hopping from foot to foot, self-conscious; small boys with sleeked hair being pulled back into family groups as they tried to seep out among the gravestones.

How many times had he parked his car round the corner and crept up unobserved on such a gathering, slipped unnoticed into a back seat, a rear pew?

It was all so familiar, but it was as unreal as a dream, the car was depositing him at the very gate of the church, people were stepping back to allow him passage. He was watching one more tableau as remote as a film show, but he was the hero. All these overdressed people, most of them unknown, were there because of him, Neil Carter, they were following him with their eyes as he walked to the front of the church, to an appointed place.

"Are you all right, Neil?" Alex's kindly face, close to his, looked slightly anxious.

"I'm fine, don't worry." But, for a few moments, he had been walking, kneeling, sitting, unawares.

Cathy's people were overflowing from her side of the church to his. He must have seen something on his somnambulistic way up the aisle, because he had a memory of crowded colour on the left, and of a few unfamiliar pieces of it being introduced among the predominantly dark sprinkling on the right. Well, so far as he was concerned there were only Alex and Aunt Dorothy and her daughter Mary and a few friends and colleagues. Cathy hadn't all that many more friends, but her mother and father had. And a large number of relations . . . Anything worth having was worth an effort, and he must make some gesture to the incredible good fortune of winning Cathy. And offer some thanks. *We thine unworthy servants do give thee most humble and hearty thanks . . .* They probably didn't say it in those words any more.

Neil Carter getting married. The whispering and rustling all round him was the sound of the jungle hemming him in, the yellow finger of sunlight across the chancel steps was the only light that could penetrate the imprisoning branches of the jungle trees . . . Even if he turned and blundered back the way he had come, he couldn't be sure of reaching daylight. Marriage to Cathy. *Cathy.* Panic, when even the name Cathy was in vain. What was he doing? There was still time . . .

Head down towards his knees, gradually, he hadn't given anything away . . .

A hand on his shoulder, imperiously tapping, breath on his neck. A reverberating whisper. "Hello, Neil darling." Cousin Mary, when he swivelled round, smiling a grotesque smile. But what was surprising him was his own smile, there instantly in place, and his own voice, whispering back how nice it was to see her, implying it was nice to see her absurd smile, her little hat, too narrow for her broad face, too far forward for her age and image . . . He had to turn back because his own smile was threatening to become a laugh, he must tell Cathy he had had to turn away from his cousin Mary because he was in danger of laughing in her face . . . Cathy. *Dear God, I thank you.*

Where was Cathy? A glance at his watch showed him she should be standing at his side.

"She's late."

"They're always late." Alex's cheerful confidence made him feel belligerent.

"I didn't know you were an authority."

"For goodness' sake, Neil. Anyway, stand up, they're here."

He hadn't noticed that the drifting organ sounds had stopped, recognizably resumed. He was on his feet, holding the wooden rail in front of him with both hands, finding he was gripping it as Alex nudged him into the aisle. There was a hiccupy intake of breath, undoubtedly Winnie, marking the soft progress of the feet, then a waft of air, a scent and, as he turned his head, Cathy beside him, her eyes and smile assuring him through the veil that he was part of her mystery.

Dearly beloved, we are gathered here in the sight of God and in the face of this congregation . . .

The schoolgirl on the bed would never stand in the aisle of a church and hear those words . . . Not now, not *now*.

The vicar had fallen silent, he was waiting to see if anyone was going to object to the marriage of Neil James and Catherine Ashley. But no one could, he hadn't left any unfinished business and Cathy was wearing her white dress honestly. Even though most of the people on his side of the church wouldn't believe it, with him for the bridegroom. But he didn't know if it was honestly, he didn't know her short history. He had always, even while feeling unreasonable and unfair, hoped she would tell him she had never . . . But she hadn't told him, she had even once said, in some forgotten context, "Neil, I've lived, I've—" and then he had put his finger to her lips, because he didn't want to hear what she might be going to say. The girl so alive in that bar, so dead on that bed, who had known her short history?

. . . and, forsaking all other, keep thee only unto her, so long as ye both shall live?

"I will."

I will do my best.

"I will."

Her response was very quiet. Her father had stepped back into his pew, one of the little bridesmaids gave a sharp child's cough, Cathy's hand was in his, cool but trembling slightly, he was repeating what the vicar was saying, he heard his voice calm and firm. His own hand was trembling when Cathy took it, her voice was as steady as he thought his had been. He didn't know what she thought about the words *and obey*, because he had insisted that she didn't say them. He had forced her to obey him by leaving them out. Only now, he saw the irony . . .

He had Cathy's left hand, was sliding the gold band smoothly down the fourth finger, holding it there.

With this ring I thee wed; with my body I thee honour; and all my worldly goods with thee I share.

He and Cathy were kneeling, he had put out his hand again, to steady her among her draperies. The vicar was holding their right hands between his, wrapping them in his stole.

I pronounce that they be man and wife together . . .

He was married. Cathy was married. She was married to him. She was walking with him as his wife behind the vicar, between the short rows of choir stalls, to the altar, together they were kneeling down.

Lord, have mercy upon us.

He would have no mercy upon himself if he didn't love her, comfort her, honour her and keep her. As she had been kept by her family. There was surely something wrong in that family where the schoolgirl . . .

Our Father, who art in heaven . . .

And on whom the vicar was calling to bless him and Cathy, and then announcing a hymn. *Love divine, all loves excelling.* It was right, of course, to be reminded . . .

He helped Cathy to her feet and they stood side by side as the hymn was sung around and behind them, while the vicar talked kindly to them for a few minutes and he held Cathy's little finger among the folds of her dress . . .

Kneeling for the last time, receiving the final blessing, divine seal of approval, trying to remember the phrase to repeat to Cathy, standing for her favourite hymn.

The Lord's my Shepherd, I'll not want . . .

The case was wrapped up, they'd arrested Frank Tate, his dabs were everywhere in the bedroom and also on record, so that he'd had to run the awful risk of coming back for his engraved cigarette lighter. He'd seemed confident at first that the alibi he'd told them about, the vital alibi for that Sunday morning, would hold up, but the man couldn't even be found . . . It was all straightforward, and yet he, Neil, wasn't happy, he kept remembering those few unprovocative words, the words of the schoolgirl looking so superciliously at the camera in the photograph they'd got from her father . . . *It makes me sick, the way I can never get away from home, never, never, never.* The true voice, he'd thought at the time. The true words? And the lad had said—eventually, when he knew it was a choice of charges between murder or interfering with an underage girl—he'd said he had to retrieve his lighter because the girl had told him she was a minor and he didn't want any part of *that*. It could be true, as it could be true that he'd left early not only because there was someone else coming, but because of that revelation of the girl's. Hadn't so much left, in fact, as fled. And not from a body, from a living girl . . .

Anyway, he wasn't missing any of the action by being away from the office for a week, it was all wrapped up . . .

The New Forest. He hadn't been there for years . . .

They were leaving the chancel, and Cathy's arm was pressed between his arm and his side. Following the little cousins behind them now were Sir Roderick McVeigh with Aunt Dorothy, Lady McVeigh with Alex, the procession was breaking up as it entered the vestry, as the choir resumed distantly singing. The first photograph was being cajoled from them as they stood by the register, he was lifting the veil from Cathy's face and kissing her nose as he laid the veil back. She was lovely and normal and down-to-earth, smiling at him reassuringly, asking for a second picture with the vicar in it. The name of Neil Carter was significantly adjacent to the last appearance of the name of Catherine McVeigh, to the names of his mother- and father-in-law and his stepbrother, Alexander Carter. The procession was re-forming, and he and Cathy, to a bright burst of Mendelssohn, were leading it up the aisle between the smiling, encouraging faces. They were responding, he to the left across her glance, she to the right across his.

The photographer had gone out of the vestry door and come round to meet them. As he helped to arrange the folds of Cathy's dress, Neil noticed it for the first time, plain and white, and the chaplet securing the veil, and realized she was almost beautiful. He told her so, and as she smiled at him the photographer went into action.

"Now—Mummy and Daddy. And your brother." And then a wider circle, and a wider.

At the gate there was confetti, and a stinging handful of rice in his face. Old customs, he supposed, died harder in the country . . .

In the back of the wedding car sitting bolt upright side by side and hand in hand, proceeding slow and stately back to Grange Hollies. Very slightly embarrassed.

"I was just thinking—your father that night on the landing at
Westcote Gardens. Asking me if I'd keep an eye on his young
daughter. D'you think he minds?"

"Neil, what an extraordinary—"

But he was already correcting himself. "I mean, is he really
pleased? Eight years, and I'm hardly—"

"If you're going to talk like that, Daddy's not even a baronet.
He was knighted for services to industry. Don't be ridiculous,
Neil. Anyway, Daddy likes you."

"I know your mother likes me. Your father . . ." Always so
scrupulously polite, so unspontaneous.

"Daddy takes knowing. I know him, and he's happy because
I'm happy, quite apart . . . Neil . . ."

They turned to one another on an instant, and the embarrassment dissolved. Neil just had time to adjust the chaplet before
they were helped to alight outside the house.

No sooner inside, than the process of tidying Cathy being carried further by more competent hands. Getting into line for the
reception. Self-conscious, then amused as he looked towards the
dining-room door.

"Mrs. Dorothy and Miss Mary Parsons!"

Of course they would be first, he could have opened a book on
it; Aunt Dorothy, who was the younger sister of Alex's mother—
he couldn't even muster a blood relation—and her daughter,
Mary, who had been jealous of the beautiful second wife but was
now embracing her son so vigorously her absurd hat met a moment of acute danger . . .

"Mr. and Mrs. James Duffy. Mr. and Mrs. Peter Sinclair."

Cathy's sisters and their husbands. Penelope Duffy a larger,
louder version of Cathy, cheerful and inconsequential, embracing
him in a smother of wholesome eau de cologne, going on about
some domestic catastrophe which had almost made them late.
Angela Sinclair dark and thin and perhaps secretive like the father, her untidy husband in appropriate contrast, as Penelope's
neat one to Penelope . . .

"Mr. and Mrs. George Larkin."

Detective chief inspector. His chief. Who hadn't been in his
mind for a moment all day. He hadn't looked for him in church,

hadn't listened for his foghorn nose blow. There was, after all,
another life.

But there was Juliet.

"Well, Neil, very nice. Very nice, eh, Amelia?"

"Very nice, George."

Small, shapeless Amelia Larkin, full of pleasure and excitement, jerking forward to peck him and Cathy on the cheek, the
chief, in a morning coat a little too small for him, saluting Neil's
wife with a smacker on the cheek, pumping Neil's hand up and
down. He was still pumping as Neil turned to indicate to his
mother-in-law the significance of this inelegant duo . . .

"Miss Elizabeth Prince."

Sharing their landing, Miss Prince had taken a roguish interest
in their choice of flat.

"Mr. Carter, Miss McVeigh, oh dear, silly me, Mrs. Carter of
course . . ."

"Neil and Cathy, Miss Prince, Neil and Cathy."

Miss Prince's hat surprisingly becoming, even saucy, hiding
most of the overpermed hair, her hand convulsing on his arm as
she decided not to lean up and kiss him, blushing as he leaned
down to kiss her . . .

"Mr. David Hughes."

His amiable sergeant, looking wonderingly at Cathy as he took
her hand. No doubt trying to imagine how such an attractive
girl . . .

And all the time, McVeigh friends and acquaintances, some of
whom he would no doubt sort out over the years. *Over the years.*
It was astonishing, perhaps the most astonishing thing of all, the
way he welcomed, seized on, every indication of ever after, he
who had once been uneasy at the thought of weeks and
months . . .

"Miss Winifred Eccles."

Winnie was on him before he had brought his thoughts back to
the room, kissing his ear as he hastily turned his head, devouring
Cathy with both bare arms.

"Gosh, Cathy, I almost didn't make it, the wretched bike
wouldn't start outside the church and if one of your dishy uncles
hadn't come to my rescue . . . I got all hot and bothered."

There was slight olfactory evidence. But Winnie was the last of the line. Cathy's chaplet was awry again, and there were variously coloured lip imprints on her cheeks and chin.

"You'll have to go upstairs, you're covered in kisses. Don't be long."

He waited with Cathy's parents for her to come back. Her father said, "You remember that night Cathy moved into her flat? I asked you if you'd keep an eye on her."

"I was mentioning it to her when we were on our way back from church. I hope you don't feel I overdid it."

He thought the meeting of their slight smiles promised some understanding. Lady McVeigh, down-to-earth and tough, was looking even more wistful and frail than was her wont. Of her three daughters, she must have been most like Cathy in her youth . . . The nearest he had ever got to thinking about marriage had been that he could only consider an orphan. But even two hale and hearty in-laws didn't seem to be disconcerting him. He stood between them as Cathy came back into the room, part of a family for the first time in twenty years, since his mother had died.

The sun was out again, and some people had taken their drinks onto the lawn. High-heel marks in the grass would be part of his memory of the day. The photographer had come round the side of the house and was there to meet them once more. In the marquee, the bridal party ranged behind a long table, looking across the flowers at the small tables filling with guests.

"It won't hurt the grass." Winnie's breathy reassurance rose for an instant above the hum of conversation, the sudden creation of a small desert by the buffet had to do with Winnie and an overfull plate. Food was being placed in front of him, the next stage would be speeches, his speech, thank heaven he never minded, although it was always harder to say a few well-chosen words than talk with a brief. He had it roughly ready . . . He was aware of Cathy watching him and he turned to her, catching her expression of happy absorption, knowing more surely than ever that she would never resent his silences, his withdrawals, hoping he would never resent hers. Doubtful, though, acknowledging that even in his casual relationships he had been possessive, his sexual pride always braced to counter real or imagined slight . . .

A throat clearing, at hand and slightly above him. Cathy's uncle John was on his feet to propose the toast to him and Cathy. As the biography of the bride, affectionate and slightly facetious, began its duet with the sympathetic laughter, Neil felt for the oblong card in his inner pocket. Not that he would use it; he knew what he would say, including the additions as Uncle John's pleasant speech continued on its way . . .

Small old West Country hotels. There were doubtless small old New Forest hotels as well. Bellfield near Brockenhurst. One of the most attractive areas of the forest. Bellfield a very small country place, and in small country places people talked to and about one another. And the college. There might even be an appropriate course . . .

For a few seconds he had a glorious vision of Love and Work flying heavenwards together like a Victorian statue. He'd have to ask the chief, of course, who despite Neil's attempts to chip away at his complacency seemed happy enough at the way the case had been opened and shut by Frank Tate . . .

And he'd have to ask Cathy, prepare for her disappointment and then control his own . . .

Cathy's hand was on his knee. There were unmistakable signs that Uncle John had almost done.

". . . and so I ask you, ladies and gentlemen, to raise your glasses to the two young people in our midst"—that was generous of Uncle John—"to Cathy whom we know and love, and to Neil whom we love for loving Cathy, and look forward to getting to know. Ladies and gentlemen, the bride and bridegroom!"

"The bride and bridegroom!"

". . . an unusual and agreeable experience to find myself in a gathering of people who are all of one mind about the subject of the meeting." He had begun to speak, was well into it, before realizing that this particular speech was vitally important, that fairly or unfairly his lifelong reputation would hang on it for more than half the people in the marquee. Gratitude above all things, genuine gratitude, for Cathy, for the wedding, for presences and presents . . . The right balance, not too frivolous, not too solemn. Light things seriously, serious things lightly. The relief was considerable, as he saw his audience enjoying what he was saying, not just putting on a show for the McVeighs' sake. When he sat down he was aware of a number of unfamiliar smiles and knew he had passed preliminary muster.

Alex spoke drily but appropriately, and read out the telegrams with all the right emphases . . . What did he know about his stepbrother, really? But what had he known about anyone before he had started wanting to know about Cathy, except for the brief, sharp spotlights he turned on the individuals he had to investigate in the course of his job?

Juliet Payne . . . He needn't say anything to Cathy today. Once he'd spoken to the chief, he wouldn't think about it again until tomorrow. He'd ask Cathy in the morning, on the other side of the rainbow-coloured divide . . .

She was whispering to him, a large knife was being proffered by the handle. Heavens, he had seen the tall white cake because he had had to dodge round it for an unimpeded view, but he hadn't looked at it, hadn't mentioned in his speech the known fact that it had been made by Penelope. He put his hand on Cathy's, and the photographer went back into action. The top two layers were lifted off and carried away, he put his hand over Cathy's again and pressed, to a subdued cheer. Penelope was leaning forward and he was making grateful signs and kissing his fingers . . .

"Neil, do you think we might just go round the tables and say a few words to people, before we change?"

"Of course."

He had paved his way in his speech and he rather enjoyed a procedure which once would have been the stuff of nightmare.

"Darling, I'll just have a word with my governor."

"Of course, darling. I'll just have a word with Winnie."

He was wondering how he could separate husband from wife, but the chief had seen him coming, was on his feet and moving to the very edge of the marquee.

"Well, Neil, you off to the West Country now?"

"In the morning, governor. That is, we're off in the morning, but I—"

"Has to be the West Country, does it, Neil?"

"Sorry, governor?"

But he knew, in the nick of time, that he and the chief had each been set to ask the other a favour. He'd been lucky that the chief had moved first.

"It just occurred to me, Neil"—the chief looked away across the tables—"that if you still have this totally perverse feeling about that child's killer not being her killer, you've got the opportunity of prowling anonymously round her home ground. It's only a village, and the personnel's small. Also it happens to be a rather attractive part of the world. The Fallow Deer at Bellfield—"

"Cathy wanted to go to Devon and Cornwall."

"Ah yes. I see. Well, never mind, just an idea." The chief brought his eyes back to Neil and innocently smiled.

Neil smiled back. "On the other hand, we do hope to have a large number of years and holidays in front of us, and I happen to like the forest. Good hotel, is it, The . . ."

"Fallow Deer. Very good, I believe, Neil. It was you I was thinking of. It'd have been pretty clear to a blind man that you haven't been too happy this week. So far as your work's concerned, I mean, of course." The chief's smile stretched to a beam. "And I know you've regretted not getting to Knightsbridge in time." This was one of the chief's low ones, but he went on quickly. "Not that you did anything, of course, which wasn't perfectly correct, but when a decision turns out tragically, however just, one tends to feel one wants to be extra specially thorough—"

"Yes, governor, yes."

"So I just thought, Neil . . ." said the chief apologetically.

"All right." He'd learned his lessons in sounding grudging from the chief himself. "If Cathy agrees."

"If your wife agrees, of course. If she does"—the chief reached into a pocket—"I've got a list of the New Forest personnel here to make things simpler. Take it anyway."

"Thanks, governor." Neil took the second copy of the Xeroxed list—the first was in his wallet. He'd thought he might just find a moment to go through it again.

"Better go now, Neil, your wife's waiting. Have a good time wherever you decide on. The Fallow Deer. I'll see you in the office a week on Monday."

The chief started to lumber back to his table and Neil went upstairs with Alex, Angela and Cathy. They parted two by two on

the landing. It seemed the normal thing to do, but as he shut the
prescribed bedroom door Alex murmured, "The last time you'll
be going your separate ways."

"Alex, will you be our first guest?"

He thought his brother came slightly to attention. "Neil, of
course I will. And just let me say—if I'd been able to dream up a
Cathy for you, I couldn't have done as well."

"Thanks. I wish *you* . . ." Alex had never married, but there
had been rumours of a long devotion ending in death. He didn't
know, he had never asked, and not from reticence.

"Not now. It's all right now. But I'll come and stay."

He was absurdly pleased. "We'll get in touch as soon as we're
home. Cathy'll be glad too."

He knew her well enough to know that she would be. When he
was ready, he asked Alex what he should do.

"Talk to me, or be silent with me, for another quarter of an
hour, then go and see if she's ready."

Neil talked extravagantly about unimportant things until Alex
interrupted him and told him it was time. He knocked on the door
of the room Cathy and Angela had disappeared into. Cathy
opened it to him. She was wearing a slip of a dress and sandals,
and she was alone.

"You didn't have to knock, Neil."

"I felt as if I did." There was a double bed in the room. "I
wonder if a bride and bridegroom have ever succumbed to one
another at this stage, locked the door and left the guests to eat and
drink a bit longer?"

"I suppose some bride and bridegroom, somewhere. Not these
days, though, they're much more likely to have . . ."

She had looked away from him and he took her by the shoulders.

"Cathy! You're not sorry we've waited?"

Solemnly she met his eyes. "Not sorry, Neil, of course not, just
— well, just a bit shy. I know it's silly, but I don't suppose I'd be
shy if we'd—"

"I'm not sorry you're shy. Come on, two hundred people are
waiting for us."

They said their particular good-byes in Sir Roderick's study, then their general ones at the front door, where there was more rice and confetti, and a couple of tin cans which Neil stopped to detach in the farther reaches of the drive, using the large pair of scissors supplied by the practical Alex, and just managing to get back behind the wheel as the feet came pounding.

"Foiled!" he reported, as the driving mirror showed him the four young heroes panting, frustrated, in the disappearing gateway. Cathy didn't respond, because she was weeping. She wept, luxuriously and it seemed happily, half the way to London.

CHAPTER 4

"I know it's silly Neil, but I feel—well, I feel as if I was a visitor. Here in London!"

"Now you mention it, so do I. It's our new status. You've never been in London as a married woman. I've never been here as a . . . married man."

"Hadn't you better say, 'married to Cathy,' and quickly?"

"It seems to be all right. A married man, a married man. No gooseflesh, no palpitations. But 'married to Cathy' sounds better."

He had at last forgotten Juliet, but her face was gazing at him solemnly from a newsagent's hoarding, already fraying at the edges. Last week's news. Still, for him, stop press . . .

He was aware of several pavement faces grinning at the car, and he drew up short of the flats, beside the small memorial garden where he had asked Cathy to marry him. A sticker on the near side of the car announced that a marriage had taken place. It peeled off almost without trace.

"That's little brother Robin's work, Neil, I know it is."

"No damage. And some innocent pleasure for those we've passed by. Do we still give ourselves away?" If they went to the New Forest, it couldn't be as a honeymoon couple. He turned to study her. Skin and hair as dazzling. Eyes as bright. Something less than relaxed in her manner.

She said breathlessly, "Let's go in. I'm glad we're spending our first night at home."

Two things, now, he was hoping to deny her.

"Cathy . . . I think it's time to let you into the plot your father has hatched."

"You can't hatch a plot by yourself. What have you and Daddy—"

"I'll tell you, I'll tell you." He thought she had relaxed with the distraction. He, as well. "Your father has given us an extra wedding present. A night—tonight—in a rather good hotel."

"But we said we wanted to be at home tonight."

"A very special hotel. A family joke of an hotel."

Mystification, memory, happy surprise, chased each other across her expressive face. "I know. I know! Daddy really is amazing, fancy him thinking of *that.* Like Bertie Wooster, I have an Aunt Agatha. Had. And like Bertie Wooster, I was taken to tea at the Ritz. When I was about five, I suppose Daddy told you. I was dazzled by all the marble and glitter and I said that when I grew up I would live there."

"I don't suppose you still want to do that. We'll just take overnight things and I'll put the car away and we'll get a taxi and then in the morning a taxi can bring us back here to collect everything and get the car and start off for—for the country . . ."

In the bedroom they stood looking at the new wide bed where Cathy had spent a week of nights she had refrained from saying much about.

Neil found her hand. "If you'd really rather be here . . . ?"

"No, of course not." Her hand was trembling.

"I'll go next door, then, and sort my few things out for tonight."

He didn't have to make an effort, at that moment, to leave her. He picked up his case again and went out; for the last time, he crossed the landing to the other flat, which had been his own. When he was inside, he stopped and detached the front-door key from his ring, put it down on the old kitchen table he had sold with the property. As he went slowly into his bedroom, he realized that somewhere at the back of his mind he had been fearful of these moments.

His bed was bare. That morning, in sole possession of the two flats, he had taken his bed linen across to the other one and stuffed it into Cathy's washing machine. Then taken all his clothes and put them in her spare-room cupboards. Those pictures and ornaments and bits of cutlery and crockery of his which he wanted to keep were already across the landing. The pieces of furniture which were to go into store had labels on, the rest were to be sold.

Everything would be gone by the time they got back, and anyway he would no longer have access . . .

His holiday case was packed, he had only to transfer a few things to the small one. When he was ready, he walked round the flat for the last time, perhaps testing himself to see if it hurt. It did hurt a bit, if he thought about the past, but his main sensation was surprise, that all his memories of this place were private, solitary. He had ranged far and wide, but he had always returned alone.

His key ring no longer felt swollen, with Cathy's key as replacement rather than addition. A new sort of normal life had begun.

"I asked Alex if he'd come and stay with us." It was the first thing either of them had said in the taxi. "Be our first guest if you haven't anyone else in mind for the honour. Was that all right?"

"Of course. I'd love to have Alex to stay. I'm so glad you thought of asking him."

"He'll be an easy guest."

"I'm sure."

"Robin must come if he would like to."

"Not so easy. But I'm glad you wouldn't mind."

"Of course not. I'll take him to the Yard."

If only they could break through this ridiculous formality.

She murmured in the hall of the Ritz, as the porter preceded them to the lift, "I'm glad you didn't try to persuade Daddy not to do it. Do you mind if I ring—"

"The moment we're upstairs. I did just dissuade him from booking us a suite. I thought we'd rather like to have dinner downstairs, and then . . ."

"I'll feel sorry for all the women."

"I'll feel sorry for all the men."

The room was enormous, with one large bed. When the porter had left them, Cathy, to Neil's relief, abandoned her demure tread and danced round the room. "It's like another wedding cake. Look at all that moulded icing sugar on the ceiling."

Downstairs, in the jolly splendours of bar and restaurant, she was still almost her exuberant self. But, by the end of the meal, Neil was aware again of the unfamiliar shyness between them.

"Are you tired?"

"I don't really know." She gave an uncharacteristic trill of laughter. "Are you?"

"I don't think so."

"I don't think I want any coffee."

"Neither do I. Let's go."

He set a fairly swift pace out of the restaurant, into the lift. He was almost beginning to be afraid, almost getting angry that he was. He didn't touch her in the lift, nor she him. They walked the turns of the corridor in silence to their door.

"Nothing really to unpack." Neil seized his case, flung his pyjamas at the bed. It was rotten, to feel like this because he had done what Cathy's church would approve of, not what he had once so much wanted to do. "You use the bathroom first."

She went in with an armful of things and closed the door. Her father, disclosing his plot, had said as drily as he said everything, "Don't know if it's a particular night for young couples or not, these days, but I'd like you and Cathy to spend it in a particular place." He'd been thinking, most of the time somewhere, what sort of a night it would be, but he had never thought of this awkwardness, this stupid embarrassment.

At least it was taking his mind off Juliet Payne.

Cathy came out of the bathroom wearing a matching nightdress and negligee. They didn't seem like her at all. "The bathroom's yours, Neil."

As he went in, she was sitting down solemn-faced at the dressing table; he could see her reflected between the two candle lamps as she slowly brushed her hair. At least she was in bed when he came back, he had half expected her to be curled up in an armchair. She was already well over to one side but made an unnecessary gesture of moving up. She murmured, "I've taken this side, but I don't mind which I have."

"Neither do I." He was staring at the ceiling, actually wondering what it would be best to do, when there came a choking breath. "Cathy, what is it?"

"It's nothing, I just suddenly started to laugh at us, we're being so silly. Neil, come here!"

Some time later, in his delighted astonishment, he pulled the bedclothes away to gaze at her nakedness, before shrouding it in the crushed folds of the chiffon still adhering to one shoulder. "Aren't you glad now that we waited?"

"Y-e-e-s. But somehow one doesn't like feeling a special case."

"You are, Cathy, you are."

"I think I was jealous of all those experienced women for whom you *didn't* wait."

Juliet Payne, at fifteen, had been an experienced woman. But he didn't think she had ever lain relaxed and affectionate in a man's arms.

"What is it? Neil?"

She had seen that smallest of shadows without even looking at his face. He wouldn't have to hedge, prevaricate. He would simply have to tell her. And then ask her.

"I was remembering that dead girl. I didn't tell you—but if I'd answered her SOS right away and not ten minutes later I might have saved her life. We wouldn't have got involved with the car crash and we'd have got to that flat more than an hour earlier. They say she'd only been dead a short time." He had to stop speaking.

She moved her arms in gentle encouragement, but didn't try to dismiss his grief.

"Neil, how awful for you. But ten minutes—you *mustn't*. I think ten minutes was very quick. It was just fate, terrible fate, you *mustn't* blame yourself. Your chief doesn't—"

"No, oh no. But I can't help feeling . . ."

"Of course you can't. But at least you caught the murderer."

"So it seems. But I'm not entirely happy about that, either. No, lie still, I'll tell you . . . I know it all looks straightforward. Frank Tate was certainly going to break in to get his lighter if we hadn't opened the door, he'd certainly spent the night with her. But she said something to me on the telephone, the only thing she said in what must have been her own, schoolgirl voice. She said, 'I can never get away from home, never, never, never.' I can't forget those words. And there was another thing she said, at the beginning. 'Someone's on the way that I'm afraid of.' Now, she surely wasn't expecting Tate back. And even if she was, she could hardly have been afraid of him, she'd just spent the night with him of her own free will. And Tate swore he had an alibi."

"He didn't, though, did he?" Cathy had learned more from the papers than she had learned from him. He hadn't wanted to talk about it.

"No. That is, the man he said could help him does exist but he couldn't be found, he wasn't at home or anywhere else. So Frank Tate's going to stand trial, the evidence seems overwhelming. I just feel . . . uneasy somehow. I've been chipping away at the chief all week, but of course I've just sounded absurd. However, you know when I spoke to him just before we left the marquee—"

"Yes?" Her body had tensed.

"He reminded me that she lived in some sort of adult education college in a picturesque village in the New Forest, and he told me that the village has a very good small hotel called The Fallow Deer. Cathy, do you think . . . Does it absolutely have to be the West Country? Tell me honestly—"

She didn't even hesitate.

"Honestly, Neil, if you'd like to do a bit of snooping round the New Forest I'd adore to come with you. If you'll let me snoop round the scenery a bit as well."

"Cathy!"

She sat up and leaned on an elbow, looking solemnly down at him.

"Don't misunderstand me, Neil. There are some things I'll dig myself in on absolutely *immovably* if I think I'm right and you're wrong. It just happens this isn't one of them. I'd like to go on a case with you, and I'd like to go to the New Forest."

Despite Juliet Payne, he had never been so happy. "I don't misunderstand you. And I must tell you the whole truth. Cathy, if the chief hadn't asked me if I'd consider going to Bellfield, I was going to ask him if I could. Subject to your agreement. I wasn't holding out on you, the idea only came to me while Uncle John was speaking." It had started to come to him at the altar, but he would not tell her that. There was nothing, now, which he felt he was unpardonably withholding.

She laughed. "Uncle John did go on a bit. Neil, we've only booked one hotel, so we'll only have one hotel to cancel."

"Darling . . . We could see if there's a course on at the college during the week. Not only is the girl's father the principal, her aunt is one of the lecturers."

"I know, I read about it."

"So long as it's not advanced physics or Sanskrit made easy."

"We could basket-weave, or paint plates."

"We could bird-watch. Study faces through binoculars."

"We can't be on our honeymoon. I mean," she said, hugging him, "we can, of course we will, but other people wouldn't wear it."

"No. Oh, Cathy, you are marvellous. And I won't of course let on what I do for a living. As it is, we may be a bit suspect, strangers trying to get into the college just after it's been so notoriously in the news. They may think we're the press."

"We might disarm them by being as honest as we dare. I mean, we can say we've heard of the college because of its having been in the news. We're on a New Forest pilgrimage—one of our mothers was born and brought up there—and we thought we'd see if there was a course for good measure—"

"Better make it my mother. Easier, with her being dead."

"Neil . . . Yes, you're probably right. Funny if there was a course on our wonderful policemen."

"Busman's honeymoon."

"It's going to be that anyway, whether or not we pay for tuition."

In the past he had known laughter as the way to passion, but not laughter like this, nor passion so all-encompassing, sweet instead of bitter in its end, leading to the sleep not of welcome oblivion but of contentment.

Cathy woke him, bending over him and touching his eyelids, and his transition from the vacuum of sleep to the awareness of his waking life was part of the surprise of the night. They lay companionable, blowing the bubbles of their thoughts and following them about the elaborate stucco of the ceiling until the waiter arrived with breakfast.

CHAPTER 5

Easy enough to cancel the hotel at Beer. Easy enough, to Neil's pleased surprise, to book a double room at The Fallow Deer in Bellfield. But with Frank Tate's arrest the press contingent which had rushed down to the New Forest had doubtless rushed back to London, and there couldn't be more than a couple of "in depth" people left. He had saved the trickiest to the last, and saved it for Cathy, as likely to sound the more innocent of the two of them. There might well not be a reply on a Sunday, though, from Bellfield House's listed number.

But a woman's voice answered almost immediately, defensively.

"Bellfield House!"

"Hello," said Cathy. "The college?"

"Yes."

"Forgive me ringing on a Sunday, but I thought it was just worth a try . . . You see, my husband and I"—she cast her eyes down before Neil, mockingly coy—"are on our way to the forest today for a short holiday, and we just thought there might be a midweek course—"

"You . . . just thought?"

Neil, sitting close enough at hand to be touching Cathy's hair, could hear what the harsh voice said.

"No," said Cathy sweetly, "it wasn't quite that, I'll be honest. We heard about the college because of its— troubles and that gave us the idea. We thought your work might still be going on. I'm a teacher myself, and although my school has broken up I know some schools and colleges have another week before the Easter holidays, and we just thought we would ask you . . . Forgive me, I know you must be sick of telephone calls—"

"Sick of sick telephone calls. I'm sorry, you must forgive me.

We still find ourselves expecting the worst. Yes, we do have another week of courses before Easter. Mrs. . . ."

"Carter. Mrs. Neil Carter." Neil's name hadn't appeared anywhere in the media. Cathy stuck her tongue out at him. "We're staying tonight at The Fallow Deer." No need, they had decided, to tell their background lies until absolutely necessary. "What courses . . . if there are still vacancies," said Cathy humbly.

"We have Beginner's Bridge. That's limited, but we could squeeze in another two. Then there's a larger course on Stress in Modern Life. And there's an Introduction to English Furniture." On the last words the hard note left the voice, and Neil had to lean towards the telephone. "Spaces on both those." Now the voice sounded weary.

"That's marvellous. Could you hold the line a moment while I ask my husband—"

"I'll hold."

"Thank you." Cathy put her hand over the mouthpiece. "Bridge. Stress. English—"

"I heard. Not bridge. What do you think about the other two?" He didn't know if he was asking Cathy's opinion because he was going to be a good husband, or because he wasn't sure which of the remaining two options more appealed to him. He did know that it didn't matter to him which they chose, that for this first morning pottering about in a room together in dressing gowns, nothing mattered beyond the closed door. Even Juliet Payne.

"Stress sounds intriguing, but we're all right this morning. English Furniture? We're both interested—"

"English Furniture."

"Oh, Neil, what a bonus." She put her right hand into his as she took it from the telephone. "Are you there? We'd like to go on the English Furniture course, please. When does it start?"

"Tuesday afternoon at two-thirty. Until Wednesday evening. It's residential for Tuesday and Wednesday nights, but if you're staying at The Fallow Deer we're only down the road."

"Do most—students—stay at the college?"

"Yes, but—"

"Then, I think we'd like to stay too. I went on a course once in Surrey and a couple of people who lived near and had decided to go home at night regretted it and wished they'd booked in. So if we could please have a double room."

"All right, Mrs. Carter. If you can confirm—"

"May we call in in the morning?"

"That will do very well." The voice, no longer suspicious, was deep and rather attractive. For the first time, it hesitated. "I'm Bertha Hazell." There was a sigh. "I suppose you've read . . ."

"I'm so sorry, Mrs. Hazell."

"Thank you. I am in fact tutor for the English Furniture course. I look forward to meeting you and your husband."

"And we look forward to meeting you." Cathy had blushed scarlet, dropped her eyes again. "Thank you very much. Goodbye. Oh, Neil. I feel so deceitful!"

"Darling." He cupped her anxious face in his hands. "That's only the first time you're going to feel like that. Now's the time to stop if it's really going to upset you. They won't have relet our rooms yet in Beer." He didn't know whether he was gambling on her loyalty, or whether he was really ready to do what she preferred. It was extraordinary how becoming aware of someone else was making him more aware of himself, if only to realize the obscurity of his motives.

"No, of course we won't stop. It's just that she sounded so nice once she'd given up being on her guard. Neil, it must be awful. There's just one thing I think you might do. Tell me absolutely all you can about Juliet Payne and her family."

"Of course I will." Of course, it was only fair. And it needn't go anywhere near his secret shame. "I'll tell you in the car on the way down. I'm going to forget them until then."

"I'm glad we waited to have breakfast together." Cathy was throwing the remains of the toast and croissants out to the sparrows on the stone ledges. Immediately, they became a descent of pigeons which blocked out the light. Hastily shutting the window, she danced back to him. "And it's going to happen every day. Most days for the next thirty years will be a bit rushed, but there'll be Saturdays and Sundays. She sounds interesting, Mrs. Bertha Hazell."

"She's taboo until we're on our way." It was marvellous that it should be Cathy, rather than he, who was thinking about the work he hadn't been able to resist asking her to put up with. Thirty years of rushed mornings with Saturdays and Sundays would be nothing like enough.

On Hammersmith Bridge she told him to start talking.

"There isn't all that much to say. Seeing that one of the girls is dead and the other missing and they neither of them left any explanatory notes."

"But how could it happen? I mean—"

"It's the most incredible thing, but the most understandable in an extraordinary sort of way. The other girl, Carol Hardman, alias Gail, used to live in Brockenhurst; she went to Juliet's private day school in the forest for a few terms—long enough for the girls to become best friends. They kept in touch, and when Juliet started those London music lessons a couple of years ago it was arranged for her to stay with the Hardmans—"

"Neil! Thirteen!"

"Oh, it was all as it seemed at first. The Hardman parents were at home and Juliet and Carol were under supervision. Then, about eight or nine months ago, the parents went to the States because Mrs. Hardman is American and her mother was ill there. Hardman *père* is a journalist and he transferred to some New York paper, I can't remember which. Carol goes to day school in London now, and was supposed to be dividing her nighttimes between a couple of aunts there, and spending her spare daytime hours in the parental flat if she wanted to. Cathy, each aunt thought the girl was staying with the other, and of course she *did* stay with one of them most of the time. But every fourth Saturday night at least, when Juliet hit town, it was always the *other* aunt where they were . . . And as each aunt was related to a different Hardman parent, they didn't really know each other and didn't liaise. So you see—impossible and pretty well foolproof at one and the same time."

"And that final weekend?"

"Carol really did spend the Saturday night with one of the aunts. That wouldn't have been very popular, but a friend of the Hardman father was there for dinner. The particular distraught aunt involved told us she asked Carol to invite Juliet as well, and Carol told her Juliet wasn't coming up that weekend. I suppose

Juliet hadn't seen why her fun should be spoiled too. Carol went back to the parental flat about three o'clock. The police weren't advertising their presence there—to see what she or anyone else would do. She let herself in, calling 'Marilyn'—Juliet used to get a train home from Waterloo just before five, so Carol would expect her still to be there. The police told her what was what and then—"

"Neil, she didn't see . . ."

"Oh no, Forensics had finished with Marilyn *in situ* by that time and she'd been taken away. Carol was hysterical, though, not surprisingly, and when they were bringing her down to the police car she broke away and she . . ."

"Yes, darling?"

"She ran away."

"But—she must have been found by *now.*"

"Actually no." He could hear the annoyance in his voice. Even with Cathy he was annoyed by association to have to say that a sixteen-year-old girl was still untraced after a week, with her face on every other hoarding. As if on cue it appeared beside them as they rejoined the river at the Mortlake curve. *Have you seen this girl?* A less memorable face than Juliet's plumper, more vaguely defined, younger despite the year's seniority. But, like Juliet's, scrubbed and schoolgirl. He'd wanted them to touch up some of the photos—she might have gone to ground as the nymphet. In which case an off-duty policeman with this photo in his wallet could have passed her, saying not tonight Josephine . . .

"There she is," he said sulkily.

"A weaker face," said Cathy judicially. "I should think it was Juliet who had the idea."

"We don't know, of course, but from what we've been able to get out of the aunts between handwringings, it appears that Carol *did* stay with one or other of them most of the Saturday nights Juliet wasn't in town, which suggests Juliet as the prime mover."

"Neil, did they actually . . . Did they pick men up?"

"They did indeed. I've spoken personally to at least three young fellows who enjoyed Miss Payne's favours. I wish I could stop talking in this flippant way. I don't feel flippant."

"I expect it helps, it's so awful. The poor father. And Aunt

Bertha, too. Perhaps even worse for the parents of the other girl. Not knowing."

"Better to have your dog run over than disappear. I'm doing it *again.*" They had stopped at a pedestrian crossing, and the man passing the bonnet of the car returned his grimace. "The parents have flown over, of course. They're in the flat."

"Poor, poor things. Does what's-his-name—Tate—have anything to say about Carol?"

"Not a thing. He's ended up with Marilyn—Juliet—the last three Saturdays she was in London, but he'd only seen Carol briefly the first two times, not at all of course the third."

"I wonder why Carol ran away? I mean, she's got an alibi for the murder."

"A watertight one. I think it must just have got too much for her. To take in what had happened, what their behaviour had brought about. And the thought of her parents being told could have been the last straw which made her bolt."

"What have the police done so far?"

"We're dragging the Thames. It's a big thing to do. We're stumping round from door to door with photographs and questions. We're standing on railway stations and at bus depots. We're doing what the police do anyway 90 percent of their time."

"Oh, Neil. I expect you'd like to have been stumping around too."

"I'd rather be down in the forest. I couldn't have managed that if I wasn't on leave, so it's worked out very well." He took his eyes off the road for the first time since he had begun to tell her the story, to exchange grins.

"I do wish I could help you. I don't suppose they know whether the people in Bellfield have alibis or not, with Frank Tate having presented himself right away?"

"That's an exceedingly helpful remark. They've taken formal statements, of course, which included times and whereabouts, but they won't have followed them up. The girl's father was at the college all Sunday—no doubt about that—and Aunt Bertha was spending the night with a friend in Southampton. Came home after breakfast."

"Any Bellfield person who could have been in London that Sunday morning?"

"Two people with Bellfield connections who *were*." They were approaching the wandering river again, Twickenham Bridge. The blue areas of sky were steadily growing, the prevailing cloud whitening and dwindling. "Bertha Hazell's stepson lives and works in London. A solicitor. Very rarely comes to Bellfield. Bachelor. Thirty-two. Peter Cowley, tutor in English at the college, has a mother who lives in Bayswater. He was on holiday staying with her at the very time. Bachelor. Twenty-four."

"Neil . . . I see why you don't feel certain about anything."

"It isn't so much the setup, it's those words the girl said. In that voice. 'I can never get away from home.' She says that at the same time she tells me she's expecting a visitor. And then dies. Cathy—"

"Juliet's mother's dead, isn't she?"

"Died of leukaemia when Juliet was ten. That could have a bearing."

"I wonder how well Aunt Bertha took her place?"

"I think they saw quite a lot of one another. Bertha Hazell lives in a cottage near the college and does a few administrative things about the place as well as lecturing occasionally. She married quite late and her husband died about three years ago of a heart attack. I've been the London end the whole time, remember, I haven't met any of them either, or else we couldn't be doing what we're going to do now." They were sliding onto the M-3. When they came off it, at its other end, they would be in Hampshire. "There's an awful lot to find out. The men who went down weren't really looking for anything and they felt they were being made to waste their time."

"A pity you couldn't have been at the funeral. On films at least, funerals are awfully useful occasions. When was it?"

"On Friday."

Cathy was shifting about in her seat. "Neil, they'll be so *raw*. Still saying, 'This time last week.' Well, they'll only just have stopped saying it. But—it's not as if it's straightforward grief. I mean, a living schoolgirl, then a dead— a dead *strumpet*."

It mightn't be just himself he would be worrying about, afraid of getting too involved.

"We'll decide where my mother lived when we get there, see the lie of the land."

"I think," said Cathy, putting her hand on his, "that she died quite recently."

"When I was about sixteen I went to see where she'd once lived, because she'd told me about it. Her first home after she was married, a sedate little road in Ealing where she'd been especially happy. To make sure we don't get into difficulties, we'd better say she lived in Bellfield when she was a child. That'll give fifty years or so clearance. But the instinct's the same."

"Yes. How old would she be, Neil?"

"Sixty-two." His mind had really only one good picture of her, sitting under a tree in the garden of her second married home, himself playing round her feet and occasionally glancing up for the reassurance of her smile. Whenever he looked at the picture, it hurt for a minute, but less, he now discovered, because of Cathy. "In a way, now, I'm glad she isn't sixty-two."

"Age didn't wither her. I know. I hope Mummy never gets really ill . . . All right, Neil, your mother lived in Bellfield when she was little—say up to ten?—and we'll discover where when we discover the college and the cottage?"

"That's it."

"How long have we been married?"

"Two years? With you only looking eighteen, it can't really be any longer."

"I shall be twenty-four next birthday. Neil, I hope happiness doesn't make one callous. I only seem able to feel these people's unhappiness the far side of it."

"I'm glad to hear it. I don't want you to feel the unhappiness of the people in this business. It's not part of our lives." He wished he wasn't speaking so emphatically. "It's just one of the puzzles I'm paid to solve. 'And, besides, the wench is dead.' "

And, perhaps, preparing to haunt him.

He could feel Cathy looking at him, and because he was dodging into the third lane to overtake an enormous vehicle apparently overconfident of its capacities, he directed his reassuring grin at the windscreen. They gave in, then, to the steady roar of speed, and were off the motorway, at a comparative snail's pace, when Cathy broke the silence.

"Funeral on Friday. Sunday morning now. Neil, don't you think it would be useful if we could somehow get into Bertha Hazell's cottage while there's still a chance of her stepson being there? I mean, he must have come to Bellfield for the funeral, and might stay on until Sunday evening."

"Of course it would be useful, but I can't see how it could be managed. We'll have to tread very, very carefully. Too many coincidences and they'll be on to us. They'll be hypersuspicious of everyone as it is. I don't mean they'll suspect me of being a policeman, but they'll all too readily believe that I'm a journalist."

"What *are* you?"

"Cathy, you are indispensable as workmate as well as wife. I hadn't thought. Tell me."

"What else do you know about?"

He pulled a face. "Nothing. My work's my hobby. I might have chanced the law, which has rubbed off on me here and there, if it wasn't for that precious stepson—and possibly someone or other on one of the courses. Can't be an academic subject, because of the college. A writer would cover a multitude, but it's a bit close to the dreaded journalism. Army, accountancy, architecture, butcher, baker, chiropodist, dentist. They're all much too risky, all need chapter and verse. If I'm a doctor, someone will have a stroke. If I'm an electrician, the fuses will blow. If I'm—"

"Then, be a civil servant. Nobody ever wants one of those in the home. And if you think, nobody ever asks a civil servant a question about his or her work. They just say, 'How interesting,' and change the subject. And if you just look dreamy if any one *is* bold enough, they'll probably think you're Special Branch."

"Darling, you're . . . Of course, I'm a civil servant. And you're—"

"What I am. No need to change. You can direct any fire on me. You know what I'm like on my own subject when I get launched."

"I should say that makes our alibis, at least, unbreakable. You're incredible."

"And you're generous to let me see you're impressed. Where are we now?"

"The A-33 isn't very forthcoming, but Winchester is some-where on our right. One of today's losses for the traveller, if not for the town, is that you don't see the places along the way any more, you have to leave the road."

"Winchester's lovely. I spent a weekend there once with Penel-ope."

"You can spend a weekend there with me. Not on this trip, but you can."

"Neil, that's the sort of thing which makes it so marvellous. Suddenly realizing that things one did before, and enjoyed, are going to be a hundred times better. What about Bertha Hazell's husband?"

"I only know she married a man a good deal older than herself when she wasn't in her first youth, and inherited the stepson whose name I can't recall unless I reach into my pocket for the list the chief gave me." He might even tell her, eventually, that there were two lists, because it was funny.

"It doesn't matter, probably easier not to know than to pretend you don't. Is—was Juliet Payne a bright girl?"

"I think so, I think it came pretty easily to her. And she'd been in the same form as Carol at the forest school, despite being nearly a year younger. I think her music potential was really something. I saw the old man who taught her. He's a nice old bloke who was making himself feel awful because he couldn't help being even more upset about her loss to music than about her death." The old boy had actually wept, sitting there in front of Neil with his thin yellow hands up to his face, rocking and weep-ing, while his German wife made anxious guttural noises in the doorway.

At least, if his hunch about Frank Tate was right, they wouldn't have to come back to that old couple—there was hard evidence they hadn't stepped outside their flat that Sunday morning.

"How did he come to start teaching her?"

"He came to the college to give a weekend course—he's retired from that sort of thing now—and heard Juliet play. He told me she used to infuriate him because she seemed to value her gift so lightly. But even without Frank Tate, we know the old man didn't hobble across London, infuriated or otherwise, to take her life." He suddenly felt suffocated. "Cathy, let's not talk about Juliet and her world any more just now, unless you think of something else you really want to know."

"Of course not, darling, I do tend to forget that you found her. I'm sorry."

"Don't be silly. And it's not that."

It wasn't, of course, any more than it was his delay in answering Juliet's summons. What was troubling him was the fact that he had made it possible for her to issue it, that he had been a victim of himself, rather than circumstance. All right. He knew. No point in probing the spot, he couldn't heal it that way.

They were back on the motorway again, skirting Southampton to the north. The sky was enormous, the cloud reduced to a few cirrus trails. He had another sudden sense, this time of elation, born of the space.

"Cathy, what time is it?"

"Almost twelve noon."

"That's perfect. We register at The Fallow Deer. Have a drink and lunch. Take a stroll and look around us. Just what the civil servant and his wife would be expected to do in view of the reason for their visit."

"We've got to find The Fallow Deer first."

"I think we'll come upon it as we come upon the village. The college is the far side of the village so far as we're concerned now, and Bertha Hazell's cottage is this side, so we can start looking out for it as soon as we turn off the Lyndhurst-Brockenhurst road. Ivy Cottage. Bob Ryan says it's set back a bit, just past a similar little place which is on the road."

"That could be your mother's childhood home."

"It could. Bob said they both appeared pretty ancient, but I don't know how sound he is architecturally. It might be some rustic thirties dream."

"Then, we'll find somewhere else to fit. Neil, we're in the forest. I'd forgotten the ponies came in so many colours and textures."

They had left the motorway at Cadnam, and the road to Lyndhurst—"William Morris did some work in the church, Neil.

If we have a chance . . . And Alice is buried in the churchyard"
—and beyond towards Brockenhurst was edged with woodland
and pony-dotted clearings. Although they were looking for the
sign to Bellfield, the lane off was so embowered they overshot it.
Ivy Cottage was preceded by Rose Lawn, and The Fallow Deer
had chairs and tables in the garden.

CHAPTER 6

"Shall we have a rest before we set off?"

"There's nothing I'd like more, but you saw for yourself, Neil, how difficult it was to come straight down to lunch. Our only chance to get a glimpse of that stepson is to present ourselves in the area of the cottage absolutely right after lunch." Cathy looked thoughtfully through the window, where several lunchers had adjourned for coffee to the small, sunny garden. " 'Have a rest.' It'll be as good a phrase as any."

"Oh, Cathy." Neil's eyes slid past the two adjacent tables where the two solitary men in ostentatiously informal clothes were alternately concentrating on their plates and papers and glaring at one another. Perhaps the head waiter had a particular sense of humour, or had had enough. "You're right, of course. If we *do* see him, may we reward ourselves with a rest before getting ready for dinner?"

"Even if we don't. I suppose it's madly unlikely. But we should be there."

"I know. Ten *al fresco* moments for coffee, and we'll be on our way."

Outside, at a table on the edge of the lawn, they could talk more precisely.

"D'you think any of Juliet's family have been lunching with us, Neil?"

"Not the family, from what I remember of the photos. But I'd take a bet the two gentlemen eating alone are members of opposed sections of the press engaged in trying to woo the family to give them the Real Story. I wonder how well they're doing."

"Not well at all with Bertha, surely. Oh! Thank you."

They were silent as the waiter retreated.

"That man was far too kind and interested," said Cathy when

he had disappeared behind the creepered wall of the hotel. "I hope there weren't any bits of confetti on the bedroom floor."

"I don't suppose there were." Neil was amused by the naivety of the idea that Cathy, with her dazzling smile and tip-tilted nose and fair cap of hair, would be no subject for kindness and interest unless she was a bride. "He just got infected by our good humour. Look, darling, don't *not* do anything you want to do. Don't for goodness' sake leave my hand alone when you want to take hold of it. I hope we'll still hold hands when we've really been married for two years. Just try and remember not to talk about yesterday." He didn't really have to say that; he had already discovered that Cathy, in the midst of her sometimes breathless precipitation of words, was impeccably discreet.

"It seems such ages ago, it won't be so difficult."

Cathy shrugged into her cardigan as they went through the front door of the hotel onto the narrow main street of Bellfield. A March wind was rising, scudding the thin cloud across the sun, turning the bow window opposite from mirror to plain glass and revealing the contents of a small general store.

"To your right, sir. Round the two bends and just past Mrs. Hazell's." The large, friendly porter was standing on the step between them. "A weekend cottage, Rose Lawn is now. And not every weekend, either. Thirty years, Mrs. Richardson had Rose Lawn." But not fifty. Neil and Cathy looked towards one another at the same moment. "Richardson. That was the name I couldn't remember when you asked me before your lunch. I'm ashamed of myself; Mrs. Richardson used to come in for her lunch every Sunday like clockwork. Same table. Nice, quiet lady. 'Good morning, Bert,' she'd say. If I wasn't in the hall that moment, she'd come and find me. 'Good morning, Bert.' Maybe Mrs. Hazell has the key, but I shouldn't bank on it. Weekend people, who come in here about four times a year as if they owned the place. Mrs. Richardson'd have been really upset about what's happened in Bellfield." The porter, already close enough for Neil to be aware that he had been chewing garlic, bent his head against Neil's ear. "You'll have heard . . ."

"I'm afraid . . . yes."

"Those two in the dining room. From the London papers.

Won't get anywhere with a family like the Paynes. Or Mrs. Hazell. Caught one of them trying to bribe one of the kitchen staff. Well, mustn't keep you from your good work. You ring Mrs. Hazell's bell, she won't mind. If she's got that key, she'll let you look around. Mustn't keep you."

"Nor we you," said Cathy politely. The three of them were several yards along the road.

"See you later." Reluctantly Bert turned back. Neil took a gulp of air. Cathy skipped a few steps ahead of him on the narrow granite pavement, turned and waited for him as he came up to her. "I don't suppose we can go on being so lucky. D'you think we really could ring Mrs. Hazell's bell?" She took his hand as they turned the first corner.

"I do now, yes. But on form so far, she should be in the garden."

Someone was. As they rounded the second bend they could see the movement, up and down, behind the intermittent screen of shrubs and bushes set just inside the low boundary wall of Ivy Cottage. The gate gave on to a small muddy delta quickly narrowing to a cart track over a field. The passage of tractor wheels showed in the mud, had probably caused it. Three pieces of granite had been placed for negotiating the corner of the delta by those wishing to attain the gate. In enforced close contact on the last one, Neil and Cathy stood with unimpeded view of the garden worker, jabbing a boundary bed fiercely with a hoe, bending down to cast uprooted weeds on or near a pile at the edge of the lawn, so energetically absorbed that for a few moments she was unaware of the spectators. But when, stretching up and sighing, she turned away from her task, she was confronting them over the low gate with a speed Neil found disconcerting in so tall and well made a woman.

"Yes? What do you want?"

It was the voice as it had been at first when Cathy had telephoned, reinforced now by unfriendly eyes and a generous mouth drawn in. Bertha Hazell was handsome on a large scale, with a strong-boned face and shiny brown hair lightly flecked with grey. The hair, straight and simple and caught youthfully into a slide, showed Neil the girl she could have been, before making him more aware of her middle age than if she had worn a sophisticated style.

"Mrs. Hazell, it's all right." Cathy had spoken while he was still searching for the best words. "Neil and Cathy Carter. Installed in The Fallow Deer and informed by the hall porter that you live next door to the cottage where Neil's mother lived when she was little. That's why we've come down, actually, we lost her quite recently . . ."

As Cathy talked, and squeezed Neil's hand apologetically, Bertha Hazell's mouth eased and widened, the hostility dwindling in her eyes. Not quickly, but she must be growing used to being on her guard; the past week would have been a long one.

He hoped Cathy wasn't feeling too bad about what she was doing so well; he was having a few twinges himself. More as Mrs. Hazell relaxed.

"What a coincidence!" The warmth of her voice, now, showed that the comment was to be taken at its face value. Cathy and Neil mumbled agreement.

"We wouldn't have dreamed of disturbing you," said Cathy, "even though the porter said you wouldn't mind if we did." It took Neil all his self-control not to give in to his curiosity and turn to see what she looked like while she dissembled to such perfection. "But we couldn't resist coming straight along after lunch to look at Rose Lawn, and when we saw you . . . Forgive us, but we knew it must be—"

"Yes." Bertha Hazell sighed again. "Fortunately newspaper photographs aren't very precise, but there were one or two television confrontations. What am I thinking of? Please come in."

They had to gamble. Cathy, making no move forward, knew it too.

"Oh no, really, Mrs. Hazell." Neil brought to bear the smile which had stood him in such stead. "Sunday afternoon!"

"We won't come in now, really," said Cathy. "We'll be seeing you at the college in the morning. At least I hope so."

"You will, but you must come in now, I insist." Bertha Hazell's large hand wrenched the gate towards her, out of Cathy's fingers. "I'm afraid there's no one at Rose Lawn this weekend." The three of them were standing on the narrow path which went straight to the open front door. "The people who own it now don't live here, unfortunately, and the poor old house is empty most of the time. Not that they don't look after it," amended Mrs. Hazell. Generous, thought Neil, even at such a time. "They keep it up well, but they just hardly use it. They don't leave a key with me, either. Which I suppose saves me an ethical struggle." She flashed them a short-lived but powerful smile. Her teeth were very good. Neil noticed that the large but well-shaped brown legs below the denim skirt were bare but for minimal ankle socks. A type he would have guessed, anyway, didn't feel the cold. "I don't see why you shouldn't peep through the front windows, though. If they were coming down this weekend, they'd be here by now. And you can see the back garden quite well from mine. Do come in. We'll have some coffee."

It was the moment to yield.

"You're really awfully good." Behind Bertha Hazell's retreating back, Neil squeezed Cathy's hand. "The biggest optimist in the world couldn't have hoped for such luck."

Bertha Hazell was dragging herself out of her anorak, putting it down on a hall chair with one sleeve pulled inside out, looking at Cathy.

"I expect you'd like to keep your cardigan on, Mrs. Carter. Come in."

As they followed her into a small, pretty room, the sun came free of the cloud and shone on their faces. Neil thought he saw an expression in Mrs. Hazell's which he would ask Cathy about afterwards. Relief? There was certainly suppressed tension.

Footsteps sounded overhead.

"My stepson. He came up for— for the funeral, and he's catching a train back this evening. It's a very good train service," said Bertha Hazell, tears suddenly running down her cheeks. "No point in driving when you can get on at Waterloo and off at Brockenhurst. Juliet—"

She shook her head, but her attempt at a smile twisted into a grimace. Cathy put her arms round her. "Don't try to be brave all the time. You can't."

"Thank you." The words were just audible. Bertha Hazell fumbled in her pocket and produced a large handkerchief. "We'll go outside and I'll show you Rose Lawn before we have coffee."

They followed her out into the hall again, where she stopped, cleared her throat and called out.

"John!"

"What is it?" The answering voice was without expression.

"Visitors. The right kind. Will you come down in ten minutes. I'll be making coffee?" For a few seconds she listened to the silence. "John?"

"All right." Perhaps, now, there was exasperation.

"He's putting his few things in his case. It's been good of him to stay over the weekend . . ."

Bertha Hazell was leading the way to the back of the house, out of a door beside which was another, open door revealing the kitchen. It was old-fashioned but looked tidier than Neil would have expected.

The back garden was small and the sun had already left all but one corner. Neil noted the fact with disapproval; when he and Cathy bought a place with a garden, the sun would shine on its private side until it set. It amused him to realize that a few months earlier he would have been unlikely to notice the position of the sun vis-à-vis a garden, much less to have an opinion on it.

Bertha Hazell was by the beech hedge, bending and peering.

"Luckily the beech doesn't get going yet and the old leaves aren't much of a screen. Well, I don't call it lucky usually, of course, but, as I've said, they're hardly ever down. Here, this is a good place."

Dutifully, Neil first as the son of the woman who had lived the other side of the hedge, they applied their faces to the space Bertha Hazell had enlarged. The garden was much as her own in size, shape and aspect, but there was a pool edged with reconstituted stone on which sat a contemplative, red-capped gnome.

"I don't think my mother would have gone for the little man," said Neil, "and I'm sure for what she said there must have been trees in her day." That seemed a safe if sad assumption. "But it's such ages ago."

"The Willoughbys have taken some trees down," said Mrs. Hazell. "I couldn't bear it, I went out for the day until it was all over.

At least they took them out, didn't lop them—I suppose they made it a bit too dark. But I was sorry. Now we'll go and have a look through the front windows."

Resolutely she led them down the narrow gap between the cottage and the hedge, across her front lawn and over the three granite stones. The gate of Rose Lawn was more accessible, giving on to the narrow footpath which they had followed from the hotel.

"Are you sure?" asked Neil doubtfully. Cathy, with her sense of fitness, would say nothing, it not being her mother.

"Of course I'm sure." Bertha Hazell breathed heavily on a diamond-shaped pane, rubbed vigorously with her elbow. Neil took the place she yielded. An open door within helped to illumine a small, dark room which seemed to be full of red-toned reproduction mahogany.

"I don't suppose you approve the furniture," said Neil, risking an unnostalgic comment.

"No, Mr. Carter. And it doesn't sound as if you need an *introduction* to English furniture."

He turned round as slowly as he could make himself, hiding his inward alarm, but Bertha Hazell was smiling for the first time in more than a flash, paying him a compliment, not being on her guard. He smiled back.

"I know what I like, as they say. And I *have* been told that I've got an instinct. But I don't know anything, really. Best to start from scratch. Especially when you can combine it with a holiday."

"How long are you planning to stay down here?"

They must have done rather well, that the first of the questions they had been dreading came out so casually.

"Only until Sunday," said Cathy as they trekked to the next set of little panes. "My husband's a civil servant, so a week's holiday is a week's holiday."

"You're a teacher, you said, Mrs. Carter?"

Cathy's response to this question took them through the rest of the accessible windows, excused Neil from needing to make more than the odd exclamation or give vent to the odd sigh. Bertha

Hazell was seizing eagerly on everything Cathy said, making him shudderingly glad he had decided on an esoteric career.

"Do ask me some questions on Tuesday," said Mrs. Hazell as they returned next door. "Ask me one at least, and get things going. I so often see questions on my students' lips, but they just can't pluck up the courage. It's usually ten questions or none."

"Of course I will. I'm sure to want to, anyway. Mrs. Hazell," said Cathy in the narrow doorway, maybe or maybe not as impulsive as she sounded, "I must say—forgive me—I think you're very brave. Oh, I'm sorry . . ."

The tears were coursing again, as abruptly.

"It's all right. I'm lucky to be able to cry. So is poor Henry. I've never seen a man cry as Henry's cried. It's so much better if you can cry. It's especially awful, you see, to find that we didn't know her. To feel that if we'd—I'd—been more observant, given more time . . . it might all have been different. I'd been aware for some time that she'd sort of withdrawn, that I couldn't get to her. But I put it down to puberty. Girls can go quiet then. Although she's passed that stage, of course . . . Remorse. It's something more than grief, because I know already that it's never going to get any easier. Forgive me."

They stood in the kitchen doorway as Bertha Hazell again shook her head, blew her nose. Then she took up the electric kettle, filled it and switched it on. "I think I've only got plain biscuits, I'm sorry . . ."

"We really don't want anything to eat." Cathy glanced at Neil. "I think I . . . read that Juliet had no mother?"

"She died when Juliet was ten. A terrible age for a child to lose a mother. There's no one else to cry—except Carol, perhaps, but we don't know what's happened to Carol." The generous mouth drew in again. It would all be a bit more bearable to think that Juliet had been led astray. "Though now I think of it I'd have expected Peter Cowley to cry. He tends to look on the verge of tears anyway, but the way it's affected him is to drive all that baby pink out of his face and make his eyes look as if they could never shed a tear."

"Peter Cowley?" Cathy looked towards Neil again. Mrs. Hazell, despite what Cathy had said, was stretching up for a biscuit tin. But by now it was clear she was trusting them, probably blessing them for existing, turning up to give her someone safe and understanding to talk to.

"Oh, our young lecturer in English." There was the sound of rending thread as Bertha Hazell secured her objective, a few seconds before Neil could take hold of it for her. Not that he, at six feet, was very much taller. "He's been with us only since the beginning of the session, I could tell he was . . . intrigued by Juliet. Well, she was an attractive child. Had a sort of . . . stillness . . . about her, a bit unusual I suppose in someone so young. I thought she was shy! I thought—"

"Don't," said Cathy. "Please don't."

"Oh, but I'm glad to talk. It's a relief. John doesn't . . ." Bertha Hazell glanced towards the door. "I'll call him again. Unless he's in the sitting room."

Neil said, taking the tray from her, "I've known grief harden faces. Sometimes there's a big effort needed to conceal it. Your young lecturer may have been very attracted to your niece."

"I don't know. He was on holiday in London when . . . when . . . He was staying with his mother. I'd rather hoped . . . the Saturday night . . . But Juliet wasn't interested. I know now why, of course—"

"Friends of yours, Bertha? Do introduce me."

The soft, dry voice from the hall made Cathy give a little yelp of surprise. Neil, who had almost dropped the tray but disguised his shock, used the corner of it to push the door wide.

"Neil and Cathy Carter," said Neil. "And not friends, really, although Mrs. Hazell has done us a very friendly service. Shall I take this through to the sitting room, Mrs. Hazell?"

"Oh yes, please."

In the sitting room, lighter now with the sun full on its window, Neil studied John Hazell as Cathy and Bertha Hazell, in concert, explained the presence of the Carters. A tall man, slightly built, dark hair receding from a naturally high forehead. Dark brows and noticeable lashes to dark eyes. Straight nose and finely formed mouth. Expression unchangingly blank as the explanation ran its course. This man would not cry. Not, according to the reports, that he had cause to over this particular death; he had known the child, but scarcely the girl. Although it was Sunday, Hazell was wearing a dark city suit. It was easy to imagine him at his solicitor's desk, but there was something about him which Neil was unable to define.

Sparked by the apparent key role of Rose Lawn, they talked about houses. John Hazell's field was conveyancing, giving Neil further thoughts about house buying. Bertha Hazell, who seemed to have moved beyond the therapeutic possibilities of Neil and Cathy's visit, took the smallest part in the conversation, worrying at the gold chain which lay close round her throat. But she spoke into the first silence.

"I'm glad John's father—my husband—was spared this. He and Juliet were such pals."

Something, at last, crossed John Hazell's face. He leaned forward. "Don't upset yourself, Bertha." He sounded irritated rather than concerned.

"I'm sorry." For an incongruous second Neil thought of a splendid beast tormented by the drover's goad, trying vainly to escape the reality of its torment, its large eyes full of bewildered pain. Cathy leaned forward too, to take hold of the hand which was agitating at the throat. "I know it's time I pulled myself together. I do assure you, John, no one on the course next week will be aware from how I behave that anything unspeakably dreadful has happened in my family. I'm glad you're both coming on Tuesday." She forced herself to smile from Cathy to Neil.

"So are we." It was a good chance to change the subject. Neil asked how many people were expected.

"You and your wife make eighteen. A nice, manageable number. There's a chamber concert on Tuesday night after dinner, and a quiz with slides after dinner on Wednesday."

"To test what we've learned?" Gently Cathy let the hand go.

"That's the idea, I suppose. But I always feel it's more of a test of me as a teacher."

"We're looking forward to it, all of it. We'll come in in the morning and pay the deposit or sign on or whatever."

"I hardly think you need do any of those things." Bertha Hazell tried to smile again. "But I shall be glad to see you, and our secretary, Miss Booth, is a stickler for all the formalities. I hope you enjoy your day off tomorrow. And that the house cuisine will measure up to the hotel, which is rather good."

"Thank you. Now we really must go."

"I must go too, Bertha." Everyone got up. "I've things to sort out and a busy day tomorrow."

"Of course, John. Thank you for staying over the weekend."

Hazell had already brought his suitcase downstairs. They all crossed the road to the Tarmacked enclave of the field opposite backed by a brick building with two grass-green doors.

"When the Rose Lawn people come," said Mrs. Hazell, wrenching at her gold chain, "they park all over this place. Sometimes I have to ask them to move so that I can get my car in or out." Her eyes were very large and dry, her voice rather loud. John Hazell asked her why she didn't go and stay at the college for a while, and she said crossly that she was all right where she was. Hazell's car was the Daimler Neil had noticed on their way along. Hazell told his stepmother that he'd be in touch, nodded to Neil and Cathy. Neil leaned into the car to look at the dashboard before Hazell could shut the door, and was aware of an agreeable scent of cologne.

His surprise made him realize what it was about Hazell he had been unable to define: the man gave off no personal waves. Acknowledging his good looks had been to admire the appearance of someone at the remove of the television screen, someone whose after-shave lotion is out of olfactory range.

CHAPTER 7

"So . . . any comments?"

"Upon what?" Cathy rolled back towards him, searing him afresh with her smile.

"Upon the Hazells," said Neil severely. "Can you imagine John Hazell in distress?"

"Never. One of your cold fishes."

"I found myself being surprised when I put my head into the Daimler and smelt his after-shave. He didn't seem real enough to smell of anything. I can't imagine him ever smelling of himself, like that wretched chap we picked up at the flat where the girl was." Eventually, surely, he would lie with Cathy and be spared thoughts of the schoolgirl dead and alone.

"Not a bit like the stepmother."

"Not a bit. I'm sure she's warm as toast. Ouch! You don't have to be jealous of Bertha Hazell, I promise you. Although I like her."

"So do I."

"I got the feeling she and John Hazell just about tolerate one another."

"Yes . . . I thought she'd break that chain of hers."

"I had a strange feeling she was relieved when we arrived. Did you?"

"Something . . . It could have been that. I think she was glad of someone to talk to. I don't suppose she can talk to her stepson. She's dreadfully upset, Neil."

"And dreadfully tense. Didn't you feel?"

"Yes, but if you're trying all the time not to break down, I suppose you would be. You mustn't see things in people because you don't feel happy about Frank Tate being charged."

"It isn't entirely that." He turned away from her and looked up at another decorated ceiling. "I keep remembering what the girl said."

"I know. But she could have been fed up about someone from home, and still have been killed by someone from London."

"I know, I know." But he hadn't seen it that way before, and he knew his dismay was showing in his face and that Cathy had turned her head to look at him. She said softly, at last, "I want you to be glad if you don't find a Bellfield murderer, not sorry."

"Oh, darling. Keep telling me that." And keep telling himself that the truth was more important than his private image. He must not let his honeymoon turn into an ego trip. Must not try to suppress thoughts of the facts which didn't support his preferred thesis. Such as the fact that Juliet had died in the persona of Marilyn, indicating the probability, if not the certainty, that the visitor she was expecting did *not* come from home.

But as he got used to what Cathy had just said, his wariness over the charging of Frank Tate settled back on him.

"Cathy, I truly don't feel happy about Tate. The girl just wasn't frightened of him, I'm sure she wasn't. She was frightened of someone or something, no doubt about that. But it wasn't Tate. He's still protesting his innocence, you know, even though his vital witness appears to have scarpered. With all the circumstantial evidence against him, a guilty person would have it much easier if he pleaded guilty. And even if Tate did kill the girl, I feel we should find out who or what she was scared of to get the whole picture. This is one of those cases where I'm glad the judgment won't be irrevocable, that the death penalty's been abolished."

It was a relief to be voicing sentiments both honest and impeccable. And he didn't want to find a murderer in Bellfield, he just wanted the true verdict on the murder he had allowed to take place. On the death of the girl he had put himself in the position of being asked to help. And failing . . .

The evening was perfect, except for one moment in the bar before dinner when he saw the stretch of Cathy's leg down from the high stool. After dinner, which was as good as Bertha Hazell had suggested, they walked in the lamplit village, and in the night they were the universe. Extended breakfast in the bedroom was no less enjoyable at The Fallow Deer than at The Ritz. Will power was necessary to reach Bellfield House by ten o'clock, the hour they had set so as still to have a day out after the enrolment formalities were completed.

There were already a dozen or so cars parked outside the ornate entrance. To right and left of the house were single-storey extensions. Neil stopped abruptly as he saw them.

"What is it, Neil?"

"Those are bedroom wings. If we're put in one of them I shan't be able to look around." He hadn't realized what he had hoped to do in the night, until it appeared he might be prevented.

"You want to snoop! It would be so terribly risky—"

"Snoop was your word. You didn't object to the idea when we were in London."

And she wasn't objecting now for the reason ninety-nine brides out of a hundred would object, to be shared so soon with other nocturnal interests. She was astonishing.

"If there's a choice, we'll choose the main building." He spoke lightly; he wouldn't let her see, after their conversation of the night before, how absurdly important it felt to him to have the option.

In the hall (it was a room, as the hall of the flat in Knightsbridge had been a room), Bertha Hazell was facing into a Palladian alcove, arranging spring flowers. She turned as their feet sounded on the black and white tiles, and gave them a wan smile.

"Good morning."

"It is, isn't it?" Neil thought she looked more haggard and drawn than the amazon who had been punishing the soil of Ivy Cottage. But his observation (rather than his experience) had shown him that it was always worse, after a death, when life was supposed to be getting back to normal. If, in this case, it was . . .

He hadn't come to stir things up again, he had come only to ensure that justice was done.

"I'll take you to the office and hand you over to Miss Booth." Bertha Hazell led the way across the hall and opened a stout mahogany door. "Don't go without letting me know, I'll be around somewhere."

The office had a long window looking down a formal garden scarcely separate from the heath surrounding it. Miss Booth for the first moments of their entry was a black silhouette against the view. When they could see her, she looked competent and uninteresting. Neil found himself wishing that her whereabouts on that terrible Sunday might be unaccounted for, and was shocked.

Miss Booth had been briefed.

"Ah, Mr. and Mrs. Carter, yes. Mrs. Hazell's Introduction to English Furniture. I'm sure you'll enjoy it, Mrs. Hazell's lectures are always popular." Was there a slightly sour emphasis? "Now, a double room in the south annexe—"

"It's such an interesting-looking house," said Cathy, "we wondered if you might have a room free in the main building. I know we're lucky to get a room at all, but if there *is* a choice . . ."

Would she ever cease to amaze him? Miss Booth's ballpoint, which had been checked in its descent to the sheets of paper on the desk in front of her, concluded its journey.

"There is, actually." The ballpoint made a note. "Mrs. Hazell had given you a room with its own bathroom, but if you really prefer the house—"

"I think we do," said Neil. "And especially if we can have our baths in a big, old-fashioned bathroom."

Miss Booth smiled. She had thin, spiky little teeth. "You can. I'll give you number eighteen. On the main landing." There was a small cloud suddenly in her face. Perhaps Juliet's room had been close to number eighteen. He could imagine that Miss Booth's manner generally was unaccustomedly subdued, but it was of course impossible to know the effect of brutal events on people one had never met before. That was where, so far as Peter Cowley was concerned, Bertha Hazell had been so helpful. Unless of course . . .

He must remember Cathy's rebuke, not keep swivelling on to baseless suppositions.

Terms were agreed and the deposit paid. The secretary asked them if they knew the forest. When they said they hardly did, she asked them how they were going to spend the day.

"Driving round," said Neil.

"And walking," said Cathy.

The flexibility of this programme appeared to be too much for Miss Booth.

"You must take the Ornamental Drive," she said eagerly, getting to her feet and coming round the desk as if to emphasize the desirability of the course of action she was recommending. "It goes through the ancient heartland of the forest and has examples of all the different sorts of landscape. Then you simply have to visit Buckler's Hard. It's just south of Beaulieu, on the Beaulieu River. It's a minute place, but it used to be a shipbuilding centre in the eighteenth century. Between 1745 and 1818, fifty-six wooden warships were built for the Royal Navy." Neil reflected, not for the first time, how little guidebook facts told one about the flavour of a place. "The museum has some beautiful models of the ships."

"Thank you," said Cathy. They hadn't been about together much, as yet, but whenever they'd broken new ground she had made the effort to find out about it, absorbing available facts but offering them to him sparingly, and only in precise context . . . He could see, now that his eyes were accustomed to the brightness of the big window, that Miss Booth was younger than his first impression of her. She had the sort of closely imprisoned hair, a French pleat at the back, which he longed to disarrange, in the interests of freedom rather than attraction. She hadn't been in the office when they'd rung up the day before, a Sunday morning . . .

The door had opened behind them, without a knock. Neil turned round.

"Miss Booth, I wonder if you can tell me . . . Oh, excuse me."

"Not at all, we're just going."

Henry Payne. Precisely as his photograph had indicated, tall, thin, slightly stooping, cardiganed, untidy. He'd been coming up to identify his daughter, but Mrs. Hardman had spared him. Neil had wondered whether she'd been afraid it was Carol . . . He guessed that grief had modified the prevailing mild puzzlement of Henry Payne's expression into the look of resigned sadness he now wore. It was easy to believe that this man had been imperfectly aware of his only daughter. Remorse, again. It was a suffocating emotion, for the spectator as well as the sufferer. And he was somewhere between the two . . .

Bertha Hazell was still in the hall, busy at another bowl of flowers.

"That was my brother Henry," she said, leaving the flowers and joining them in the centre of the black-and-white circle under the small basilica. The glassed area at the top was pale blue, crossed by one white string. "I'll introduce you when he comes out, he's only gone in to consult the Encyclopaedia Boothica." Was this, or was it not, a term of endearment? "Is everything all right?"

"It was nice of you to give us a room with a bathroom," said Cathy. "And ungrateful of us to ask if we can have one in the main house instead. Now that we've seen the house we'd rather sleep in it, and bathe in an original bathroom."

It was the warmest smile Bertha Hazell had yet vouchsafed.

"Good! I approve of that."

Neil noticed the frown of discomfort on his wife's brow.

"Miss Booth has been extolling the virtues of the Ornamental Drive and Buckler's Hard," he said quickly. "For our expedition today. Would you agree with her?"

"Oh yes! The drive goes through the centre of the forest and of course you don't have to stay in your car. All sorts of marvellous places to get out and walk and watch deer and ponies. And Buckler's Hard is—well, if you don't know it, I'll let it make its own impact." She hesitated. "It was one of Juliet's favourite places when she was a little girl." Had she decided in advance to act as if her niece was simply a lost loved one, or had the decision been made as she spoke? He thought she hesitated again, as if to make sure she had really managed it, to speak of Juliet without losing the ability to speak further, without tears and headshaking.

"We'll do both those things," said Cathy, smiling her warmest smile, which was a considerably comforting gesture. Bertha Hazell, after a false start, returned it.

"Miss Booth takes tourists round the forest for a coach company at weekends."

"How nice," said Neil inanely. He caught Mrs. Hazell's eye, and there could have been an understanding. He thought of his father-in-law.

"Which were your mother's favourite places, Mr. Carter?"

He jangled back to professionalism. "She didn't really mention names, being only ten or so when she left Bellfield. Just picnics and ponies and the sea."

"Lymington," said Cathy. "She loved being taken to Lymington."

"So did Juliet. The school . . ." He was glad to see the office door opening. "Henry! Mr. and Mrs. Carter. I've just been telling you about them."

"Of course. Yes." Neil was aware of an enormous effort. "Are you coming on Bertha's course?"

"I just told you, Henry—"

"We're looking forward to it," said Cathy. "This is our first visit to the forest. Please just let me say how sorry we are."

Neil understood it was a risk she had to take, out of the kindness of her heart. She put her hand out as the pale eyes swam. For a few seconds, Henry Payne's fingers clutched it.

"Thank you, Mrs. um . . . It's very hard. Yes."

It was the moment to withdraw. A pity not to have seen Cowley, but there was plenty of time. When they drove off, he would forget the Paynes and the Hazells and forge a memory of the day exclusively for himself and Cathy.

At Bellfield's general store, he bought a booklet which showed them that Miss Booth had not coined the phrase "ancient heartland." Unless, of course, she was the booklet's anonymous author. The photograph of Buckler's Hard excited him: one wide street of rosy-bricked eighteenth-century terraces, the roadway turf, dotted with grazing ponies, leading straight down to the river, white boats, and a green farther shore.

"A generous street down which a man must go, even if he is not himself generous. Let's go to Buckler's Hard, darling."

"One of Juliet's favourite places."

"You won't believe me if I say that for the moment I'd forgotten. I was only seeing the photograph."

"I will if you tell me. Duty and pleasure coinciding. Buckler's Hard it is." Cathy put her hand out to him without looking up from the booklet—open on a small table in the lounge of The Fallow Deer beside the coffee tray: they had not taken the risk of going upstairs. "And then on to Lymington for lunch."

"I knew you wanted to go to Lymington."

"We must go where your mother went. And Juliet's school is just outside."

"Oh, darling." They grinned at one another.

"Easily back to Brockenhurst. Then on to the Ornamental Drive."

The booklet told them that much. It was an ungrateful slight relief, when they went in search of a porter to find the most attractive way to Buckler's Hard, to discover that Bert was off duty. His colleague told them briefly, and excused himself.

"A business like this, I expect it's echoed and reechoed through the forest. I expect every porter and every barman and waiter and waitress has something to say if prompted."

"Yes, Neil."

They'd gone back to the general store and bought a proper map before starting off, and her head remained bent over it in the passenger seat.

"I'm sorry, darling, I wanted to forget about it today, I really did. I will forget about it."

"No you won't." She looked up and smiled her consoling smile. "It would be silly, you could learn some small thing. We'll still have a perfect day. Sharing a job as well as sharing time off makes me feel—well, even more of a team if possible. I mean—"

"I know what you mean. People moan about life being unfair, but you can get more than you deserve as well as less." Nobody deserved what Juliet had got.

Cathy stretched luxuriously. "We should stop at Beaulieu and see those beautiful cloister arches in the actual stone. There's aubretia climbing up them in the picture and it'll be doing that now. We should sidetrack on the way back to Brockenhurst and have a look at the twelfth-century church at Boldre. The church at Lyndhurst. We should—"

"We'll have Friday and Saturday." But it was difficult to see over the two days at Bellfield House.

"I know, I wasn't meaning really we should try and do everything today, or even on this trip, I was just enjoying the thought that there's so much. And it doesn't matter anyway, travelling in this part of the world is as good as arriving."

"Oh yes, darling." He liked the way open heath was alternating with woodland, space with enclosure, the sun shining on blazing gorse and the first intense green of hawthorn. They had to stop while two ponies slowly crossed the road, and then skirt a stationary donkey.

On a view of Beaulieu Palace they turned south down the long country lane to Buckler's Hard, a cock pheasant running before the car. It was a shock that the lane ended in a large car park, but to turn on foot into the village was to leave it two centuries ahead. There were the rosy cottage terraces, the pale shingle path dividing the turf, the green shore beyond the water.

"The width," whispered Cathy, as if loath to break a spell. "That was so they could roll the oak trunks down to the water's edge. That's a fact to collect, don't you think?"

"It is. But where are the ponies?"

"Oh dear, I don't know. There's the hotel, anyway, at the bottom on the left. And the chapel, look, it must be."

Halfway down, a church bell hung over an open front door. Through a tiny lobby, they found a cottage sitting room with a few pews each side of a short aisle and a small altar where perhaps the fireplace had been. He waited to see what Cathy would do, and she went and knelt down. The last time they had knelt together, in her parish church, seemed light-years in the past.

On his knees beside her now, he found himself trying to pray for Juliet Payne's soul. His images of her were suddenly mixed up with newspaper pictures which had disturbed him as a schoolboy, of the fashionable psychiatrist Stephen Ward being brought dead out of his London flat after overdosing himself with drugs at the height of his corrupted and corrupting activities . . . It made it worse that Ward had chosen to die without amends, but he had chosen. Juliet had had no choice . . .

Cathy's hand touched his cheek. When he opened his eyes and turned towards her, she was watching him. She said softly, "Enough, I think. Come on, down to the water."

The few moments of near darkness exaggerated the brilliance of the day. They followed the shingle path to the river's edge. The sky, still lightly whipped with cirrus, seemed enormous. The wind was gaily blowing. A sudden exhilaration made him want to run. Juliet as a child here, surely, had behaved spontaneously.

They turned together and crossed the turf. A sign hung from a wrought-iron bracket, Master Builder's House Hotel.

"He was the shipwright, Neil. Henry Adams. What a pity you haven't got Miss Booth."

The cottage sitting room here opened into the one next to it, and probably the one next to that. Oak tables and chairs were set beside an open fire still burning a sizzling stack of logs. It would be good to come in on a winter's day; winter must rampage down this open-ended street. Today it had been the garden which beckoned, glimpsed beyond its enclosing wall beside the water, but there was a barman temporarily out of work behind the long bar.

As their drinks were set in front of them, Neil said, "You've had quite a tragedy your way."

"Oh yes. Terrible." It was excitingly possible the news of Juliet's death had been a personal shock.

"We're staying in Bellfield," went on Neil. "Going on one of the college courses tomorrow."

"I think they're very brave, carrying on," contributed Cathy. Neil saw the small frown again, between her brows.

Disbelief was the barman's swamping emotion.

"That little girl . . . The four of them had lunch in the restaurant here quite often on a Sunday."

"Four of them?" questioned Neil.

"When Mr. Hazell was alive. Such a nice gentleman. He died, I suppose, two or three years ago. They made such a happy little party. When they had drinks in here before lunch, the little girl, Juliet, used to go running outside, just to look at the water, just to see if the ponies had changed places, she used to say."

The shock made Neil's hand tremble, and he set his glass back on the counter, spilling a little of his drink.

"No ponies today," said Cathy, taking his hand.

"No ponies any day now. They were biting and kicking the visitors, so they've been fenced out."

"Probably the visitors' fault." But he felt it was appropriate there were no more ponies in Buckler's Hard. "Has she— had she been here lately?"

He watched the spilled drops shrivel into the edge of the paper mat under his glass.

"Oh no. Not for a long time. But I always remembered her. I still can't believe . . . The same again, sir?"

"No, thanks, we've got to be on our way."

He didn't consult Cathy; he wanted to get outside to absorb what he had been told. They walked back up the street in silence, but holding hands. In the car she merely said, "Another nice-looking little road back to Lymington, it hasn't even got a number on our map."

They parked by the water and walked about old narrow streets of pastel-coloured houses, glimpsing gardens behind railings and pink brick walls, talking only of what they saw and creating a space of fragile but total privacy.

It was disrupted on the cobbled way up Quay Hill, when they overtook three schoolgirls giggling together, wearing the grey pullover and red-and-grey-striped tie that Juliet had been wearing in her father's photograph.

They turned into an attractive-looking pub. There were two vacant bar stools and another unoccupied barman. Cathy commented favourably on the town.

"Your first visit to Lymington, then, miss?" The bride, her brow smoothing, lifted her left hand to her face and winked at her husband. "I'm sorry, madam."

"Our first visit, yes. Although my husband's family come from Bellfield."

Reaction showed in eyes, mouth, the jerk of the head.

"Bellfield's not a very happy place just now. But you'll have heard. Everybody's heard."

"Yes, we've heard. And we've just seen some schoolgirls. I suppose . . ." For once he was glad of the piped music, muffling their words.

The man grimaced.

"A group of them was in here one day. I say group, but it was only three. She was one of them. She was the one who came to the bar to order drinks. 'Three double gins,' she said, deadpan. When I said she knew very well that I couldn't serve them with intoxicating liquor, she opened her eyes wide and said they were only dressed like schoolgirls because it made them feel young. And"—the barman visibly swallowed—"because some men liked . . .

She was the one who had them on the go all the time they were sitting there eating their sandwiches. Nothing to pin down, just a way of talking to each other which was really to everyone else. Especially the men. I was glad when they went out. Of course it's awful what's happened, but I'm not altogether surprised."

It was an effort to respond casually.

"She was . . . noisy?"

"Oh no. That was what got me, in a way. She was quiet, and she never smiled. She laughed once or twice, a hard sort of a sound, but she didn't ever smile. The others did, silly smiles. And they were too loud a bit, once or twice. But not her, although I got the feeling she was calling their tune."

It might have been hindsight, but the man had obviously thought about it. Of course, with *Tate* written on their hearts, his colleagues who had come down here right after the murder wouldn't have bothered going this far.

"I hope it doesn't do the school any harm," said Cathy. "Can we order toasted-cheese sandwiches?"

The sandwiches were as good as their aroused expectations. So was the varied course of the Ornamental Drive.

They stopped several times, to walk over sun-chequered ground among budding trees, and to watch deer through the eye-level slits of a small hide. Once, in a clearing, they came on a pure white pony lying on the ground, and watched it get up and move away slowly and apparently without fear. They each said they would remember it, and Cathy said that for her it would become a unicorn.

Neil thought they had both managed to have the afternoon to themselves. It was with reluctance that he stopped at the hotel in Brockenhurst and rang the office.

The chief was still there. The benignity of his mood was in contrast to the distant approach which was all Neil could manage.

"Good of you to ring, Neil. You're in, are you?"

"We've met the personnel," said Neil coldly, "and are on friendly terms. We join Mrs. Hazell's course at the college tomorrow."

"Capital, Neil. Have you—"

"I'll ring again, governor, if there's anything I feel you ought to know before next week."

"Can't imagine there will be, Neil, but I'll be glad if you'll do that."

"And perhaps you'll do the same for me. I've got the hotel and the college numbers in my book, just a minute—"

"I've got them too, that's all right. Going back to the hotel, are you, when your course is over?"

"We've booked for three more nights." He relented slightly. And perhaps he would do better to end on a comparatively amicable note. "It's an attractive part of the world, governor."

"Enjoying yourselves, are you? That's right. You look after her, Neil. She's a particular girl."

He came out of the telephone kiosk grinning foolishly, Cathy asked what had amused him.

"My chief never pays compliments, it's not his style. He's just paid you one."

But with the end of their afternoon, his joy was qualified.

Girls can go quiet at puberty.

There had to be more to it than that.

CHAPTER 8

"I'm sorry about there not being a private bathroom, Mr. Carter, but you did ask—"

"We did, Miss Booth. We're looking forward to crossing the landing to the old, original bathroom."

And to being *persona grata* in their dressing gowns along the upstairs corridors. It was more of a relief than he would confess to Cathy, to have succeeded in not being self-contained.

Miss Booth, standing just inside the bedroom door, seemed determined to be apologetic. "I'm sorry we start you off without lunch, Mrs. Carter. But at this stage of the term . . . Part-time staff . . ."

"Of course," said Cathy. "Miss Booth"—as the secretary at last took hold of the door handle—"may I just say . . . I think you're all wonderful. Forgive me, but I had to—"

"That's very kind of you, Mrs. Carter, I appreciate it. I'm sure Mr. Payne appreciates it. Although . . ." Miss Booth, like Bertha Hazell, shook her head as her voice forsook her, felt for a handkerchief. She blew her nose, straightened her shoulders. She might be quite handsome in a chilly way, adjudged Neil, with her hair loose. "It's the little things," managed Miss Booth, "which keep making one feel . . . I could see her just now, on the stairs."

It was an opportunity not to be missed. Cathy and Neil began speaking at the same time, and Neil gave way.

"Of course," repeated Cathy tentatively, "her room was in the house itself—"

"Oh yes. Though it's quite a small one, tucked in round the corner, beside the main bathroom. She could have had one of the larger ones, of course—there are some lovely rooms in this house." Neil and Cathy murmured their willingness to agree.

"But she's—she'd—had that little one since she was a child and she never wanted to change. It does have a view of the garden and the heath. I don't think any of us have been into it since . . . It's just as well there are staff . . . But it's hard for them, too. Nothing's been touched yet . . ." Miss Booth shook her head again. She seemed genuinely affected. "Except by the police," she added severely.

Neil decided she had had enough. And they had done very well.

"I'm sorry, Miss Booth, forgive us. You won't want to talk about it. What time do we assemble?"

"Half past two." Miss Booth marked the change of subject with a smile. It was when she smiled, when those small, predatory teeth showed, that she was at her least attractive. "The Stress course has the main lecture room, the room where we'll be having the concert and where you'll have your quiz tomorrow night, but you've got the second lecture room, which is very pleasant. Off the hall to the left, I've put a notice up. You've got a quarter of an hour."

"Your colleagues must have gone through Juliet's room," said Cathy when they were alone. She was unpacking the small case.

"Yes. They didn't find anything helpful. In fact, they were surprised there was so little. Nothing except books to give any indication what the owner of the room was like, and there was nothing out of the way among them. Of course, something, anything, could have been removed if the murderer had access to Bellfield House."

"Of course." Cathy gave him a long look. "If there was anything to remove. It's hard to imagine anyone as horrifyingly well organized as Juliet Payne leaving anything in her room which could have given her away. What do you think you'll get out of creeping into it?" The harshness of her words was entirely dissipated by the way she put her arms round him as she said them.

"Nothing, probably. But sometimes, for me, just standing in a place . . ."

He was aware, on the wide shallow stairs, of an agreeable sense of expectancy. He was always challenged by the trappings of new experience, by the chance to match up activities with the people who undertook them.

The second lecture room was a one-time small drawing room with a few prints on the walls and a good carpet. At the far end were a screen, a blackboard and a lectern, and there was a projector on a table between the two blocks of stacking chairs, their temporary air heightened by the domestic solidity of the room around them. A few of the chairs had cardigans and bags lying across them, a few had people hovering. More women than men, of course, as always on these occasions, but a selection of men nevertheless, ranging from a youth with pimples to a frail old man with a stick.

He would undoubtedly see Peter Cowley at dinner, if not in the tea break, but he was impatient. When he and Cathy had chosen seats near enough to catch the nuances of Bertha Hazell's expression, he went back into the hall.

He knew at once that he was rewarded. Mrs. Hazell was standing nearby, talking to a fair-haired young man with a clipboard in his hand and a set, resolute expression in a face colourless but for the red patch in each cheek.

Neil moved across to the notice board and waited, his back to the two tutors.

"Mr. Carter!" called Bertha Hazell within seconds. She was at his side by the time he had turned round, making a gesture of pulling the slowly advancing young man after her. "You haven't met Peter Cowley."

"No. Hello." He would make no mention, here, of the recent tragedy. Despite what Bertha Hazell had told them, Cowley had no official part in it.

"How do you do?" The big blue eyes passed over Neil unseeing, slipped beyond him. To the staircase. Perhaps Cowley, too, saw Juliet on it.

"Have you a course today?"

"Not today," said Cowley indifferently. "A one-day course on the Romantic Poets tomorrow. Nothing like enough time." He spoke automatically. His real life, Neil thought, was going on inside his head.

"Peter does have two- and sometimes three-day courses," said Bertha Hazell kindly, putting her hand on the young man's arm.

"I always think it's easier with more time. Mrs. Carter! Do meet Peter Cowley!"

"I thought I might be missing something," said Cathy demurely in the doorway. Cowley had his first noticeable reaction to the world around him: he blinked rapidly, several times.

Neil decided that the greater crispness of Bertha Hazell's manner and appearance in comparison with her morning self was caused by the flow of adrenalin at the prospect of mounting her hobbyhorse. Not only had going on with her work failed to daunt her, it had perhaps been her salvation.

"You've seen them?" she asked Cathy, nodding towards the second lecture room.

"A cross section, I should think," said Cathy. "More women than men, of course."

"Of course. As always. Well, I'd better go in to them. Join us for tea, Peter."

"Thanks." They had to walk away from him, as he made no move.

"His work doesn't help him?" suggested Neil as he and Cathy and Mrs. Hazell skirted the projector.

"Oh, it does. It helps us all, Mr. Carter. But he hasn't any work today."

The simplicity of misery. But his own adrenalin was coursing in. And it was more comfortable, in a way, when Juliet and her world were in the forefront of his activities; they couldn't take him unawares.

The last of Bertha Hazell's mature students took their places as the tutor reached the front of the class. Neil, turning casually as he sat down, was enabled to decide at once that they were a decent bunch: every pair of eyes was focused away from Mrs. Hazell's face, fixed determinedly on the as yet empty blackboard or various other parts of the room, every face bore a faint air of apology for being interested in English furniture at such a time and in such a place, as if for some insensitivity. No one was in that room, he was convinced, for any reason beyond a concern with the advertised subject.

"Good afternoon." Bertha Hazell smiled along the rows to both sides of the narrow aisle. "I'm very pleased to see you all, and I hope I can give you an agreeable two days. Now, there is one introduction to English furniture I want to offer you right away, its framework in two senses. Where it begins, and where it reaches its maturity."

Mrs. Hazell turned to the window behind her, partly obscured by the blackboard and wholly shrouded in a fine net curtain—to cut out the dazzle, or the distraction, or both, thought Neil, of the long view.

In the window, Bertha Hazell took hold of an upright chair which had been hidden by her props and brought it forward. Its three rolling-pin legs, two at the front and one behind, dictated the triangular shape of the seat; back, arms, and stretchers were all formed, as well, of lathe-turned lengths of varying thickness. The chair was of a uniform weathered oak and looked awesomely uncomfortable. Having placed it beside her lectern, Mrs. Hazell retreated again behind the blackboard and emerged carrying a very different-looking object, a delicately proportioned mahogany dining chair in the Greek style with sabre legs and oversailing back rail, chastely upholstered in a red-and-cream-striped brocade. Set side by side, the two chairs opposed each other quite dramatically. There was a small sigh from the audience.

"What a splendid start," breathed Cathy. Mrs. Hazell, smiling now in triumph, glanced proudly at her two exhibits.

"Yes," she said. "The first of these two chairs—and that is the one thing they *do* have in common, they were both designed to take the human form in a seated posture—the first one"—she laid her hand on the rolling-pin rail—"was made about 1600 to a traditional mediaeval model. Every piece of it has been thrown—that is, cutting tools were applied to each stick of oak while it rotated on a lathe, until the required smoothness and simple pattern were achieved. It is not, as you can all see, in the least comfortable." Mrs. Hazell secured her first laugh. "But at that time in our history chairs were not intended to be comfortable. One took one's ease in bed and nowhere else"—the audience laughed slightly again—"and in company, dignity was maintained at all times. The most notable English example of the turned chair is in Hereford Cathedral—a small thing in a large place, but do look out for it if you are ever there." There was a murmur of compliance, during which Mrs. Hazell transferred her proprietary hand to the brass-inlaid rail of the other chair. "This Regency dining chair, based on Greek models, is very much more comfortable, but by the early-nineteenth century one was no longer expected to maintain even this comparative formality the whole time; now there were upholstered chairs and sofas as well—although the age of lounging was still in the future. But while there were many changes still to come, these two chairs illustrate well enough that a great deal happened to furniture in the three hundred years which are to be our subject of study during the two days of our course. And not merely to furniture. What I have already said about the different ways in which people conducted themselves in public at the times these chairs were made indicates that the history of furniture is also the history of social and domestic life. And to an extent, of course, of economics. Oak gave way to walnut, walnut gave way to mahogany, because that was the sequence in which the various woods were obtainable . . ."

Neil was amazed when a bell rang and Mrs. Hazell, finishing her definition of the word *cupboard* as originally a place to put cups *on* rather than *in,* told them that tea and biscuits would be served in the bar.

"And in case you have begun to wonder what the screen and the projector are here for, I do propose to show you slides when we resume in a quarter of an hour, illustrating what I've been telling you about the Tudors and the Stuarts."

A spell had been successfully cast, the students stirred slowly, some with apparent regret. The very young man was writing down the few dates now chalked upon the blackboard. As those at the back began to leave the room, Bertha Hazell walked the few steps to where Neil and Cathy were getting to their feet.

"It's marvellous!" exclaimed Cathy before Mrs. Hazell could speak. Neil thought he noted, as her intellectual preoccupations were discarded, a weakening in the set of her mouth. Her smile, now, made him realize that her recent smiles had been part of her professional equipment.

"Thank you, I'm glad you're enjoying it. May I join you for tea?"

"Oh, please, we'd be honoured. You've given me a sort of star-struck feeling."

Neil joined Bertha Hazell in laughing his wife's comment aside, but he knew what she meant. Mrs. Hazell's performance, the evidencing of her special skill, had lent her something of the extra, objective dimension of the celebrity.

"Are those two chairs yours?" asked Cathy as they took their place in the short queue in front of the tea trolley. Awareness that their tutor had joined them brought a slight self-consciousness to the conversation of the students immediately in front.

"The early chair's been lent to me from the vaults of a museum. The keeper's a friend of ours, but I won't say who and where he is, because it was a favour. A favour I said yes to all the more readily because I thought it was rather sad the chair was never seen. The other one," continued Mrs. Hazell fondly, "is mine. It's one of a set of four which belonged to our father. I've got the other three in the dining room at the cottage."

"It was such a good way to begin," said Cathy when they were standing about with cups of tea and biscuits in the saucers and the queue was swelling with the influx of what must be the Stress and the Bridge people. Neil and Cathy were still closest to Mrs. Hazell, but other members of the Introduction to English Furniture course were moving increasingly into her orbit.

"Well," she said, taking a long draught of tea, "I always hope it will help people not to notice that my first session is all talk and no pictures."

"I didn't notice," ventured the nearest hoverer fervently, an elderly woman with grey-white hair and an eagle eye. But I like to *learn* things. As I get older I find myself wanting more and more to *learn* things. Perhaps because time's running out."

There was a deprecating murmur. Looking round the elegant room, Neil noticed a small group of people pushing two tables together, then sitting down round them to mime and argue with quiet persistence. No doubt the Bridge people. The large group which had just begun to reach the tea trolley looked generally a bit anxious and even more self-conscious than Mrs. Hazell's team. Unless, knowing they must be the group who had come for instruction on how to cope with stress, he was imagining it. Last in the queue, glumly side by side, were Henry Payne and Peter Cowley.

Neil found himself glancing at Bertha Hazell to see if she had any reaction to the sight of them, but her eyes again were full of the suppressed excitement he had seen from his seat in the class.

"Do tell me," she said, looking round those standing nearest to her, "why you're interested in my subject."

So many people hastened to tell her, she had to take them in order. The consensus of opinion was that interest had been awakened or sharpened by visits to stately homes, and by programmes on television. One or two people possessed pieces of furniture they hoped they might learn about. There was also a sense of the therapeutic qualities of lovingly handmade things in an age of mass production.

"Don't know what all that lot are doing talking about stress in inverted commas," growled the old man with the stick. "They should come in with us."

"Or consider the cat," said Bertha Hazell with a new look in her eye, a look of mischief Neil thought suited her. "Henry's cat always attaches itself to the course which uses the main lecture room. The Stress people really only need to watch Daisy. But hush, we mustn't let them hear us."

It was unlikely. The Stress people, having secured their refreshment, were foregathering in another part of the large room. Henry Payne and Peter Cowley, sipping their tea and maintaining silence, were a small separate element almost exactly halfway between the two standing parties. Neil saw Bertha Hazell become aware of them, half raise her hand, then turn with exaggerated enthusiasm to her latest interlocutor.

"Cheer up," murmured Cathy. "Isn't it rather fun just as it is?"

"Oh, darling, yes."

Of course it was; why couldn't he accept it as such? If they'd gone to Devon or Cornwall, for goodness' sake, and found an introductory course to English furniture in a stately house, he would have been totally content.

Juliet. Insisting itself onto his mind's eye again was the expressionless face of the photograph, so distressingly old and young.

The painted face, dead or alive (the two ways he had seen it), he had at least disciplined himself not to entertain.

He hadn't done anything wrong. And he couldn't do anything right for her now, it was too late. He would—*he would*—simply enjoy being with Cathy on this civilized scene.

But glancing at Bertha Hazell's face during a momentary pause in the exchange of aesthetic views, at the miserably resigned faces of the college principal and the lecturer in English, he thought there might be another reason for his persistent sense of unease. Sorrow. Bewilderment. Remorse. The emotions sometimes beaming, always glimmering, from the three bereaved. His own unique position vis-à-vis Juliet was not letting him disregard them.

The bell rang again and the slow drift back began. Turning in the doorway, Neil saw that Peter Cowley, still holding his cup and saucer, had begun to talk to Henry Payne. Their grief, he thought, was almost palpable, distancing them from other people as if it had been a wall of glass. And yet he felt sure Bertha Hazell was suffering no less. It was just, perhaps, that she possessed a special courage, or the female ability to bow to events. He thought of the oak and the reed.

But Frank Tate was a man and he hadn't broken.

Unless, of course, the chief and company had at last worn him down. Suddenly and sharply, so that he took Cathy's hand in tacit apology, he felt a stab of annoyance and frustration at being away from the heart of things.

Yet hadn't he felt that the heart of things was here in Bellfield? Didn't he still feel that it was?

Yes, he did. Despite Cathy's warning words, despite his own attempts at common sense, he still felt the answer to the murder of Juliet Payne lay with the schoolgirl, rather than the prostitute.

Which, without the prop of Juliet, did Carol Hardman consider herself to be? Where was she? It *was* worse, in a way, to lose your dog than to have it run over . . .

The man on the other side of Cathy gave a little snore and jerked to attention. Neil just caught the apologetic whisper.

"I'm very interested, really. It's just the darkness and those two biscuits."

"Don't worry." Cathy smiled at the awakened sleeper and then at Neil, taking his hand and carrying it to the narrow space between their chairs. Passing on the screen was a rich procession of sixteenth- and seventeenth-century furniture. He hadn't realized how sophisticated some of the early stuff was. No marquetry until the Stuarts, but the Elizabethans had a splendid talent for inlay into the solid wood—here, on the side of a chest, was a delicate and detailed plan of Henry VIII's palace of Nonsuch.

"Architects' designs were available," explained Bertha Hazell, "and the cabinetmakers used them. Nonsuch Palace is supposed to have been in or near Cheam, in Surrey, but no trace of it remains."

Her face, illumined from below by the strip of light shining on her typed pages of notes, looked entirely different from its usual self, its planes exaggerated to almost sinister proportions. An illustration, perhaps, of what he was doing with a straightforward, open-and-shut case . . .

"Unusual at this time to find walnut in use, as it is, with oak, in this very fine court cupboard . . ."

Isn't it rather fun just as it is?

He squeezed Cathy's hand and was seized with a suffocating desire for her which excluded all other feeling for at least two minutes, before he remembered that Juliet Payne would never again be desired of any man . . .

To hell with it!

If he could be sure that justice was eventually done, couldn't he as surely let her go?

Fretting palm against palm, he tried to relax and concentrate on the screen. He liked Mrs. Hazell's slides, he had somewhere a sense of regret that he wasn't giving them more of his attention. As the last one came up—an elaborately carved and inlaid refectory table—he and Cathy conveyed to each other their mutual awareness, but he lost her in the drift through the doors and then was trapped just inside the lecture room by a woman who wanted to know if he came from Bristol, he was so like her niece's husband's brother, who lived by the Clifton suspension bridge . . .

He took the shallow stairs two at a time, but Cathy wasn't in their room, and he got a fairly good idea of the layout of Bellfield

House as he looked for her with an increasing sense of urgency and tension.

But in the doorway of the large lecture room he had to stop and smile. The room was empty, but in the centre space formed by the disordered rows of chairs, spread out across the shining parquet, lay a very relaxed black-and-white cat.

Hoping the tutor on Stress had been as good an example to his students, Neil turned more gently back the way he had come.

"Neil!"

The room wasn't empty; in the deep embrasure of the far window, Cathy was sitting with a young man. As he crossed the floor to them he saw it was Peter Cowley.

"Come and join us," said Cathy. Her face wore that expression of hers which he always described to himself as tender. He wanted to smile again, at his joy and relief that she was once more before his eyes.

"Hello, again."

"Hello."

He noticed to his surprise that Cowley's eyes were wet and that a teardrop trembled on his cheek. He knew that this relief must have come via Cathy. She said, in a warm, quiet voice, "I spoke to Mr. Cowley about what happened. I felt . . . he might have got tired of people not doing."

"I was very fond of Juliet. I can't believe . . . It's easier, really, to believe she's dead."

The blue eyes focused their suddenly angry disbelief on Neil, but the tears were running freely. "I'm sorry," said Peter Cowley furiously. "This is the first time I've cried."

"Then, you shouldn't be sorry." Cathy put her hand on his arm and leaned towards him. "It's better to cry."

"I know. But better for me in private. I mean, it's Dr. Payne's trouble. Mrs. Hazell's. Impertinent for me to be seen crying. You know what I mean."

"Yes," said Cathy, glancing at Neil, "I think we do."

"Ought to get up to my room." Cowley was on his feet, starting towards the other door, which led, Neil now knew, to a secondary staircase. "But, thanks. Great help . . ."

"We're glad."

Neil took the vacated place, took his wife's hand and held it against his cheek. Desire had been swallowed up in a sensation of love which he knew was making his own eyes unnaturally bright.

Nevertheless, of course, they were almost late for dinner. That is, they were the last into the bar. Miss Booth, concessionary in blue velvet but with her hair still tightly fettered, was standing with Bertha Hazell just inside. Cathy explained their lateness in her appropriate breathless way, as having been occasioned by a lost and found engagement ring. After eliciting a detailed report on their sight-seeing activities of the day before, expressing satisfaction that they had stuck so closely to her suggested itinerary, and archly admitting to authorship of the coloured booklet, Miss Booth moved on. Some items of food had been disappearing from the kitchen, and the cook needed assurance that no one was suspecting her or her staff.

"Rather more than a secretary?" suggested Neil as Miss Booth left at a pace too staccato for the blue velvet.

"Oh yes. Mary's far more than a secretary. She's been here since . . . since Juliet was a very little girl . . . I'm sorry, I'm not quite ready to think about anything like that yet." Mrs. Hazell straightened her shoulders and raised her chin. In a long simple gown of some shimmering dark red material and antique pendant earrings, she was magnificent. "It's such a pleasure for me that you're here this week. Neil. Cathy. May I? Please call me Bertha out of school."

Glancing quickly at Cathy (still, after their time alone together, unbearably attractive in a sort of William Morris flowing print), Neil noticed the little frown reappear between her brows at Mrs. Hazell's pleasure in their company. The week already showed uncomfortable signs of being one in which addresses would be sought, continuing contacts pledged . . .

There was a very nice festive feeling in the bar, and several of the students, particularly the older female ones, had gone through a noticeable process of dressing for dinner. Most in evidence were long skirts of prevailingly heavy, dull-coloured but expensive-looking materials. Perhaps the thought of the baroque concert had had some obscure influence. Bertha Hazell was clearly the cynosure of many eyes. A man from the Stress course, in fact, was looking at her in a way that tingled Neil back to his professional self. A journalist, he was certain of it.

On the way in to dinner he murmured his suspicion into her elegantly decorated ear. It made him feel even more grossly a hypocrite, but at least his motive for deceit was good. And to warn her was, perhaps, one feeble form of redress.

If in fact he was doing her and Bellfield wrong.

CHAPTER 9

Dr. Payne did not attend the postprandial concert of baroque music, and neither did four members of the Bridge course—Neil saw them in the interval through the half-open door of one of the smaller rooms, intent round a card table. But even with these omissions the combined student body appeared to fill the large lecture room. The five musicians played against a bank of brightly coloured large-leaved plants which had been set up since tea and whose names Neil didn't know. The atmosphere of diffidently elegant festivity, manifested in the bar and maintained during dinner, persisted until bedtime. Neil murmured to Cathy that the evening might just be described as brilliant. They had been able to find seats from which they could watch the profiles of both Bertha Hazell and Peter Cowley, sitting together at the end of a row near the front. Once, Neil saw a smile pass between them, but he was managing at last to relax, he wasn't watching them all the time. Nor Miss Booth nearby, although when he did she irritated him by moving her head to the beat of the music.

It was the music, which he recognized no more than he recognized the plants, which in its disciplined exuberance seemed to help him impose some order on his ambiguous thoughts and release him to savour, in the moment in which it was happening, the fact of sitting discreetly hand in hand with Cathy.

"You haven't heard any of my baroque records, have you?" she inquired as the final applause died away.

"Oh darling, oh no. I didn't realize . . ." Another dimension of this woman who amazingly accounted herself his, but who would always be her own.

"It just never came up. I knew you liked Beethoven and Brahms, so that's what—"

"I like this as well. I didn't know I did, I've hardly ever listened to it before tonight. I shall like it even better at home."

Chamber music in a chamber. Sitting room or bedroom. Cathy in the new white bed, leaning forward with her arms out . . .

It even made him forget the coming night's self-imposed hazards. It was Cathy who reminded him, obliquely, when they had gone upstairs after a last drink in the bar with Bertha Hazell.

"At least I'm the only person at Bellfield House who knows you never get up for the loo during the night."

She was smiling at him and they were in bed in five minutes, asleep in half an hour. But Cathy's soft-voiced alarm had been set for two o'clock.

When it went off he was instantly awake. Instantly more alert, clearer-minded, than he had been since he had left the office. Cathy hadn't stirred and he got ready with no more light than the grey square behind the thin curtain.

"Put your slippers on . . ."

The soft, disembodied voice, ending on a drifting sigh, would more appropriately have been speaking of faerie lands forlorn or the snows of yesteryear. He gave a snort of laughter.

"Even a two-year marriage is too short for that kind of remark. But I assure you I've already got them on."

"All right, darling. I don't promise to keep awake, but I probably shall . . ."

He transferred two small objects from his suitcase to the pocket of his dressing gown and eased himself out into the corridor. Really, he had been lucky all along the line. One quick movement round one corner, and he was in the comparative safety of the enclave which contained bathroom, lavatory, and two other doors, and where, should he be observed, he would have no need to offer explanations. If he had been superstitious, he would have been inclined to think that providence was approving of the enterprise which even he knew to be eccentric . . .

His hand on the knob of the lavatory door, he looked from one cipher entrance to the other.

Tucked in round the corner, beside the main bathroom. That was how Miss Booth had described Juliet's room.

He took his hand from the door in front of him, and without

moving his feet, extended it at right angles to grasp the nearer knob. It turned easily, but the door refused to be pushed inwards. Releasing the knob, he moved his hand towards his pocket; then, grinning, shaking his head, he made the absurd gesture of pulling it towards him.

It came, revealing blackness. Neil put his hand forward into space, but he had hardly moved his head in response to this green signal when it came into excruciating contact at the temple with some sharp protuberance.

His handkerchief, wrenched from his dressing-gown pocket, just caught the avalanche of blood before it fell beyond his face. Cursing, holding the handkerchief tightly to his cheek, he felt in front of him again with his other hand. By the time it found the light switch it had already told him he had tried to enter some form of airing cupboard. The weak light revealed the widely spaced, linen-packed shelves between which he had first groped, and the metal gadget, probably some sort of heat controller, with which he had made injurious contact.

At least now, if discovered, he had an additional reason for opening unfamiliar doors—he could (and in view of the ridiculously plentiful supply of blood resulting from his encounter, he probably should) be seeking first aid.

Still holding the handkerchief hard against his face, mopping with loose parts of it at the sticky escaping drops, he crossed in front of the bathroom and lavatory to the closed door opposite.

He could neither pull it nor push it and, cursing again, he managed to tie the handkerchief round his head so that most of the still oozing blood was contained. Then he took one of the objects out of his other pocket and, with both hands, applied it to the lock in front of him. At the end of a short silence broken by whispered oaths, he pushed the door inwards.

This time he used both hands in all directions to assure himself there were no obstacles. Anyway, beyond this door the darkness was turned to grey by the uncurtained window which defined the far wall of a small room. There was enough light for him to lock the door behind him with its own key retrieved from under his feet and, when he turned away from it, make out the dark shapes of furniture.

Nevertheless, to cross to the window and close the curtains he got down on his hands and knees and edged over the centre of the carpet, making contact with no more than the fringe of the bedspread to his left.

Juliet's room, as Miss Booth had said, faced down the garden. Still on his knees, only his head above the level of the window ledge, he made sure that the movements and shadows outside were caused by no more than the slight wind and the trees in the way of the moonlight. From the same position, he was able to draw the curtains across, and then he took the torch from his pocket, turning the small beam steadily round the room. Bedside table with lamp where he was kneeling, bookcase, built-in cupboard, small desk, door, bed with white candlewick counterpane . . .

Bed only half covered by white candlewick counterpane. Bed with a hump in it, a dark head with tumbled hair pressed into the ticking-striped pillow.

Snapping off the torch, he listened motionless, his breath held, for the other breathing. Head *pressed* into the pillow, surely there was living tension in the way the body had seemed to be trying to make itself invisibly one with the bed . . .

Only his heart refused to conform to the utter silence. It banged so agonizingly about his breast, he could imagine the shock to the other person being too great. Death by fright . . .

There was nothing ambiguous in his anxiety not to find a *body* at Bellfield House.

"I don't know who you are." And he didn't know how long he had waited before speaking. He remained on his knees by the bed, watching the motionless outline. "But please don't be afraid." *And please don't be dead.* "I'm a policeman, despite indications to the contrary. I'm investigating the murder of Juliet Payne and I'm trying to make sure we find out the whole truth. I'm Detective Inspector Neil Carter of Scotland Yard"—to his infinite thankfulness the bed jerked—"although I'm here at Bellfield House unofficially. I wanted to get to know the people closest to Juliet and I wanted to come into her room so that I could see if there was anything to help us which perhaps the policemen who've already been here didn't think was important."

"Detective Inspector Neil Carter."

The four words which had brought him to this position, on his knees beside a dead girl's bed. Just before he heard them, before the occupant of the bed began to sit up, he knew who it must be. Perhaps his instincts had known it earlier, making him speak so freely, and as if to someone young.

"Carol, I'm not going to hurt you, I'm going to help you. Carol . . . You remember me. Thank God you're all right."

He waited, sitting back on his heels and aware again of his wound. Blood had caked on his neck, but the flow seemed to have been checked.

She was sitting bolt upright now, he could see quite clearly the pale round of her face, the two small dark circles of her open eyes. He didn't use the torch.

"I locked the door."

"I know. I brought something with me in case it was locked."

She said primly, "That's wrong."

"I know. I wish it was all that was wrong. Look, I was trying to find this room and I walked into a cupboard and cut my head." It was a relief to hear the suppressed giggle. "I expect I look more like a pirate than a policeman. Before we have a chat—and we must have a chat—I'll switch my torch on and you can look at me, assure yourself I'm who I say I am."

"Oh, I know who you are. I recognize your voice."

"I'm only whispering."

"I still recognize it. I . . . noticed you."

And he, he realized for the first time, and with a disagreeable twinge, had noticed only Marilyn. If he had seen Gail again he wouldn't have known her. But as he turned the beam from his face to the girl's, he recognized the schoolgirl on the hoardings.

She made a nestling movement down into the bed as he switched the torch off. "You do look more like a pirate. But you look the same."

"Good. You don't, but I won't say any more about that at the moment. I'm sorry I frightened you. You frightened me, too."

"It wasn't so bad once I knew it wasn't Juliet."

His heart resumed its acrobatics.

"Juliet . . . Juliet's dead, Carol."

HOPE WELTY TWP. LIBRARY
Box 368 · 116 E. Wait
Cerro Gordo, Ill. 61818

"Oh, I know. That's why I was so awfully afraid it might be her."

"Carol . . ." His own first crazy thought had been that it was Juliet Payne lying in her bed.

"I'm glad you're here, Detective Inspector Carter. Don't go away."

"Not yet, I assure you. We're going to talk."

He would never have another chance like this. Each of them dependent on the other's discretion, hours of the night in front of them. He wanted to start right away to ask her about Juliet, but he must ask her about herself.

"What are you doing here, Carol?" he inquired gently.

"Hiding," she said simply. "It seemed like the only possible place. Nobody would think of looking for me in Bellfield, least of all at Bellfield House, and I can eat and sleep without risking being seen."

"*Eat* and sleep?"

"Well, it is a risk, I suppose, but Juliet and I did it so often when I used to stay here, during term time there's always such mountains of stuff no one missed it when we got hungry in the night and sneaked down to the kitchen. I just use the back stairs when everyone's gone to bed. I take up enough for twenty-four hours and some milk, but there's a tap up there with drinking water."

"Up where?"

"The big attic," she whispered impatiently. "You can open the window a bit, and I sneaked a rug up too, and there's a chest with some old books. I've read about five, I can read near the window, there must be at least forty more, they're mostly novels. And I looked at the newspaper when I was in the kitchen, I saw they'd arrested Frank. I thought Frank looked quite nice, I was jealous . . ." She paused for thought, but then, as if she found this too dangerous, began gabbling again. "I come down here for a few hours in the night, it's more comfy and the key was in the lock so I can lock myself in. I go upstairs again before it starts to get light—"

"Carol . . ." He seemed to be using her name rather often, but he was still trying to absorb the fact that this girl had turned the act of hiding into a way of life. And that she had been so close at hand. "You must know that your mother and father are very unhappy," he said sharply, suddenly angry. There was no response. Her face was looking straight ahead and her silhouette was rigid. "If you think of just one thing—how can they go to sleep at night, wondering what's happened to you? Wondering whether you're alive or dead?"

"Don't. *Don't!*"

Her chest was heaving, sobs were working up to her throat. She was rocking to and fro with her hands jammed against her mouth, then flinging herself face down into the pillow. He would be able to tell Cathy that he, too, had helped someone to cry.

He waited in silence, putting his hand out towards the heaving shoulders, then remembering Gail and withdrawing it. But as the weeping continued he reached out again and began to stroke the disordered hair.

"All right, all right, Carol. You've had a nightmare of a time. And you've been clever, hiding yourself away here. Clever but unkind. You can't stay here forever, you've got to face your mother and father at some point. So why not do it now and save them any more unhappiness? Believe me, they'll be so pleased to know you're alive and well, they won't be worrying too much about . . . about what happened. I'll arrange for you to be taken home tomorrow."

His hand was thrown aside as she leapt upright.

"If you tell them I'm here, I'll tell them you're a policeman. You said you came unofficially, I suppose that means incognito. Well, I'll tell them who you are!"

"I'm not going to tell anyone you're here, Carol. And not just because you'd give me away if I did. Anyway, if you did give me away, then I certainly *would* tell them, so we're in each other's power. No, I'm not going to tell anyone, I'm going to persuade you to go home to your mother and father of your own free will. Look at it from the most practical point of view: there won't be mountains of food any more after the end of this week and you just can't stay here forever. And won't you be missing exams?"

"O-levels? All the more reason for hiding."

"Don't be silly. How did you get here?"

"I ran down the tube at Knightsbridge and changed at Hammersmith to the District Line and went to Richmond. It was as far southwest as I could get, and then I hitched a lift to Brockenhurst, and then I walked. I got in the back door just before they locked up and hid in one of the pantries until everyone had gone to bed."

"Um. Very clever, as I said, but a waste of cleverness, because what's it for, Carol?"

"It wasn't for anything. I just wanted to get away. I just had to get away. Haven't you ever felt like that?"

"Yes," he said. "I ran away from school." He hadn't thought of that for years.

"I bet it didn't do you any good. I bet they sent you back."

"They did, yes . . . Yes, I do understand. But it's time to go home now."

"I couldn't go back to the flat."

She was suddenly trembling, and he held his hand on her arm in silence until she was still again. Then, in what he thought was a reflex movement, she twisted her body so that his innocent gesture became his hand against her breast. He pulled it away as if her nipple was a sting.

"Carol!"

She whispered softly, forcing him to remember his telephone conversation with Marilyn, "You'd be warmer in here. There's plenty of room."

"No!" He found he was shocked. "There's to be no more of that. I should have thought all this time alone would have been enough for you to become thoroughly ashamed of yourself." Or, of course, to want it more and more badly.

He saw her shoulders rise and fall. She muttered, "Yes, I suppose so." Then turned towards him again, leaning forward. "But I enjoyed it," she said defiantly. "I shan't tell Mummy and Daddy that, of course, but I'm telling you. I jolly well enjoyed it. I didn't think it was doing anybody any harm. I didn't think . . ."

Her voiced choked, she was helpless with tears. He was angry with himself, that this was the first time it occurred to him that she could be near breaking point. He said more gently, "Of course you didn't, Carol. But it *was* doing somebody harm, it was harming *you*. Sex without love or loyalty, without the responsibilities which should go with a relationship, that's harmful." He was sickened as he spoke by his double standards. But he had changed, and anyway this young and tender psyche was more important than his finer feelings. "I'm not telling you off, it's not for me to do that, I'm just explaining something to you."

"I know. I wish I'd never started it. I wish I hadn't enjoyed it."

At this his heart ached for her, and he was visited by a dim imagining of being her father. But, really, he could do no more for her now by denying voice to his first preoccupation.

"Juliet taught you to enjoy it. It was all her idea, wasn't it?"

"It was her idea, yes, at first I didn't want to . . . But she persuaded me. Juliet can—could—persuade anyone to anything."

"She enjoyed it too, of course," he stated, on a hunch.

"Oh no!"

"No?"

"Juliet didn't enjoy anything, I don't think. Oh, she did when we were little, I suppose. But then she didn't."

"Then?" Very slowly and unobtrusively he moved his numb legs. He didn't want to have to repulse her a second time.

"Well, she just went sort of quiet, I suppose."

Quiet. The word Bertha Hazell had used about Juliet.

"Why did she go quiet, d'you know, Carol?"

"I don't know. If I asked her anything, she used to turn on me."

"Did this happen suddenly?"

"I noticed it after we'd gone to live in London. But I didn't see her all that often round about then."

"Why did she do this particular thing, d'you think, Carol?"

"I don't know. I'm sorry, I don't really know anything much about Juliet, even though I suppose I was her best friend. Well, I must have been, mustn't I? When I asked her why she wanted to do . . . this . . . she kept saying, 'It's fun,' 'It'll be fun,' but then she was so absolutely beastly about . . . about the men, and said she hated them. And . . . it."

"What exactly did she say? Can you remember?"

He tried to keep his sense of urgency out of his voice. He was certain he had never been nearer to the heart of it.

"She said . . . she just said, 'Why not?' And then, 'Because I hate men, probably.' I remember that because I thought it was such an extraordinary thing to say. I just couldn't understand it at all. Can you understand it?"

"Perhaps . . ." It was a reason sometimes advanced to explain the male predilection. Thank God, whatever he had done, that had never been his reason. "Why did Juliet hate men, d'you think, Carol?"

"I don't know."

"Did she hate her father?"

He felt her staring at him in amazement, digesting a new idea. "Hate her father? Gosh, no, I'm sure she didn't. They didn't make any sort of a fuss of one another, but I always thought she was quite fond of him, she used to tease him. You don't bother teasing people you hate, unless it's nasty teasing, and this wasn't."

"No. I see." Carol might be easily led, but she had some shrewd perceptions. They just might arrest her progress down the slippery slope over which Juliet had thrown her.

"Actually," said Carol, "I always thought she liked women even less than men. Oh, she was always patient with Aunt Bertha, and my aunts too, and she was always getting in touch with me, but I always thought she was . . . just . . . well, nothing, really, although she could make them wild. But she could be sort of almost hostile with women. Especially the Boob," said Carol reminiscently. "But the Boob hated her, too."

"The Boob?" He eased himself upright and sat clasping his knees. He felt the handkerchief slipping loose round his head, and that it was being kept in place by its adherence to the clot on his temple.

"Miss Booth," explained Carol impatiently. "Bellfield's treasure."

His fingertips were tingling, literally. He unclasped his hands and held them palms up.

"She and Juliet hated one another?"

"I think they were both jealous. The Boob was quite clever," conceded Carol, "and I heard her put Juliet right on something once. Juliet didn't like to be put right, especially by someone on her father's staff. And the Boob was definitely jealous of Juliet. Bellfield House belongs to Hiatus Henry—"

"Hiatus Henry?"

"That's the name Juliet had for her father. Hiatus Henry owns Bellfield House, and he started the college, and so everyone in a way had to be nice to Juliet, and the Boob came from a small sort of a place outside London and hadn't a husband or a boyfriend or anything and was always saying she hadn't got enough money and if she was at home she'd be a slave to her mother and—and, well, that was it, I suppose."

"The Boob— Miss Booth hasn't got a boyfriend, then?"

"Not at Bellfield, and I can't imagine her having one anywhere else. She's always terribly *nice* to men—you know—but I don't think they like her all that much."

"Poor Miss Booth."

"Oh, she probably doesn't notice. She may notice about Peter Cowley, though. Juliet always used to say she was keen on Peter Cowley."

"Miss *Booth?*"

"I know, it's ridiculous, isn't it?"

"Perhaps Juliet was just . . . stirring it?"

"Perhaps she was," conceded Carol again. "Which reminds me. I saw Peter Cowley that Sunday outside the flats when I got back after lunch."

"You— what?"

"Saw Peter Cowley outside the flats that Sunday. For a detective, you take ages to take things in."

"I'm sorry, you keep surprising me. I knew Peter Cowley was on holiday then in London, staying with his mother, but I didn't realize—"

"Why should you? I don't suppose anybody else saw him. He was sort of skulking down the side street, looking moody and kicking a stone."

"He didn't see you?"

"No."

"You didn't go up to him?"

"*No.* I hardly knew him. I'd only met him once, when I came back with Juliet one Sunday, and she'd taken a photograph of him which she showed me."

"You're sure it was Peter Cowley?"

"Of course, I'm sure, Detective Carter, but it wouldn't matter if I wasn't, because you've caught the murderer, haven't you?"

"Frank Tate's been arrested and will stand trial."

"Don't you think he did it?"

Conversation in the dark, unimpeded by the necessity of reading expressions or avoiding embarrassment, seemed to make very swift progress.

"I don't know, Carol. Everyone is innocent until he or she's proved guilty."

"I didn't mean that," she said scornfully. "I think I *had* better go home tomorrow."

He had to ask her to repeat herself, and she made another disparaging remark about the speed of his reactions.

He let it go, became cheerfully matter-of-fact.

"All right, Carol. I'll arrange for—"

"I don't want anyone here to know."

"Of course you don't. The best thing would be, wouldn't it, for you to meet me somewhere outside?"

"There's a way across the heath which comes out on the Lyndhurst-Brockenhurst road. You turn towards Lyndhurst when you get back on to the main road, then carry on to where you see a sign saying public footpath to Bellfield. It's a sort of lay-by where you can park."

"Half past nine?"

"I'll be watching for you. I shan't come out unless you're alone."

"I promise I'll be either alone, or with my wife. She's got short hair and looks about eighteen."

"Gosh, are you married?" She was more interested in what he had just said than in anything else which had cropped up during their conversation.

"Why so surprised?"

"I dunno. You just don't seem like it, somehow. I'd never have thought you were married. Gosh, I wouldn't have suggested, either . . ."

"That's all right."

He had known things were going too well. It took him a few unpleasant moments to remember that he'd only been married four days. "I think now I must go back to her."

She jerked down into the bed. "You don't sound very enthusiastic."

"Oh, I am, Carol, I am. I just want to be sure I haven't forgotten to ask you any important questions. You've been awfully helpful."

There would, of course, be another chance in the car in the morning, even if he decided, as he thought he would, to ask the chief to send someone to take over from him in, say, Southampton. But then the usual social reactions would obtrude.

"Have I? I didn't think I'd said anything particular."

"You have. Are you going back to the attic now?"

"Not yet, I can sleep here for another couple of hours. It was lucky I had my watch on. Although I've got a sort of instinct now about the right time to do things." She yawned deeply, turned her head into the pillow. "Good night."

"Will you lock the door after me?"

"Yes. Good night."

"Good night, Carol."

He had to stumble round the room to get his circulation going. When he got back to his own room, Cathy was reading. She scrambled out of bed and ran towards him, and in the dressing-table mirror he saw why. Hair, face, and dressing gown were caked with blood.

It was painful, removing the handkerchief, and while he told her his tale she bathed the really quite small wound and applied a plaster, assuring him from the depth of her Red Cross experience that he didn't need stitches.

CHAPTER 10

It was not, of course, as straightforward as it had seemed when he and Carol had made their assignation. He had to get on to the chief with no chance of being overheard, and he had to find a good reason for cutting Bertha Hazell's morning session, which would have been simple enough had he stayed apparently unwell in the bedroom but which would seem an insulting sort of a thing to do if he drove off in his car.

"What do you suggest, love?"

It was a bit like the problem of choosing an occupation for his Bellfield House persona, the kind peculiarly suited to Cathy's talents.

"There's a call box downstairs with a door, where you put money in. No one to listen in—on the line or nearby. Does finding Carol justify waking the chief up?"

"Definitely."

"Then, why don't you go downstairs about six o'clock and ring him? If you see anyone, it's late enough not to be suspicious. If you can get someone to take over in Southampton, it'll save you missing Rococo and Neoclassic as well as William and Mary and Baroque."

"Even if I can, what do I tell our friend Bertha?"

"You could ask your chief to arrange for you to have a telephone call at breakfast time. Let's see . . ." She was lying on her back, and in the soft light of her bedside lamp he could see she was frowning at the ceiling. More stuccoed cornices, although less elaborate than the one in the room they had had at the Ritz. In Cathy's flat, their flat, they would lie looking at a plain coved ceiling . . . He wanted to kiss her, but he must wait until she had pronounced. Her face was clearing. "Yes, you've come away with some key which they need in your office, and you've been asked to hand it over to a colleague in Southampton."

"Only one key?"

"Yes, that is a bit ridiculous . . . There should be two keys at least, of course, but the other one's been lost. So the careless behaviour is down to this colleague, rather than to you. It's not very good, Neil. I'm sure you can think of something better."

"I can't. I'll be very disappointed and I'll be back for the afternoon. Maybe even very late morning."

"If she doesn't turn up, you'll have to fill in time."

"She'll turn up. She wants her mummy."

"She's a little girl again, is she?"

Cathy was still staring at the ceiling, he still leaning on his elbow to survey her. Her face was rigidly intent and he thought perhaps she was pondering a further question.

"Yes. But that didn't prevent her suggesting that I got into bed with her."

Cathy turned her head sharply towards him. It dissolved him to see her eyes full of sorrow, rather than shock or suspicion.

"Oh, Neil, how dreadful. What a prospect for her."

"I know. One can only hope she'll have some good luck to offset the bad, and find a man to satisfy her who happens to care about her. If she does, I could just think she'd be all right. The poor child told me how much she enjoys it, and wishes she didn't."

"Is that mother of hers intending to stay in England now?"

"I don't know."

"She should, she really should." Cathy sat up and leaned across him to take hold of the clock. He detained her somewhat half-heartedly, realizing his weariness. "I'll set this for ten to six." She grinned at him. "Have you a headache, darling?"

"It throbs. I can bear it."

When the alarm bell woke him for the second time, his head throbbed less supportably and he lay feeling sorry for the bridegroom whose honeymoon was being so insensitively disrupted. He felt sick as well as tired.

Cathy was leaning over him.

"Shouldn't you go and make that call, Neil? It's gone six o'clock."

He groaned deeply as he moved.

"Are you all right?"

"No. I don't have to get dressed, do I?"

"Better not. And you don't have to have an explanation for making a telephone call, it's your own business. The dressing-table mirror's got a sharp corner, by the way. You walked into it last night."

"Somewhere the far side of my private pile driver, I love you. I shan't be long."

He had another moment of regret on the back stairs, as he blinked through the long window at the delicate, bird-accompanied morning, that he should have any awareness beyond that of being in the New Forest with Cathy, but by the time he had slipped apparently unobserved into the telephone kiosk, his only thought was of what he would say to the chief and of the chief's reaction. And then, as he dialled the chief's home number with the customary reflex sinking of the heart, that he hoped the chief's wife wouldn't answer.

He always hoped this—she was an effective barrier between her husband and the world out of office hours—but this time there would be, he was certain, an additional indignation on behalf of Neil's bride at so unnatural a devotion to duty; the picture of amiable excitement Amelia Larkin had presented at his wedding had been a phenomenon.

"Yes. *Yes.*" It was the chief.

"Governor, it's Neil Carter. My regrets at ringing you so horribly early, but I've found Carol Hardman and I want to hand her over to someone in Southampton." He said it all swiftly against the background of grunts. Then, as these ceased and no voice followed, went on to give himself the rare pleasure of making a self-defensive statement which he knew could not be opposed. "I can only take her as far as Southampton, because I'm committed here all day. I'll have to get out of half the morning session as it is. Can I be telephoned here at the college about nine for a pretext to get away? Governor?"

"All right, Neil." He always had to admire the economical way in which his chief could recover. "I'll see to that. Where did you find her, then?"

"Asleep in Juliet's bed." That was the sentence he had most looked forward to offering the chief. After it, he could be magnanimous, not point up his superior's second setback by allowing a silence. "Look, governor"—through the round window of the kiosk he could see a woman wielding a vacuum cleaner—"it probably isn't wise to do too much talking where I am now, I'll tape a report upstairs and hand it over to whoever you send. Carol gave me one possible fact which may interest you."

"All right, Neil," assented the chief grudgingly. "It'll probably be Bob Ryan and a sergeant."

"The parents?"

"Possibly, possibly. By the way: hope this kid won't try to compromise you. With her history and both of you in a bedroom—"

"I'm pretty sure she won't, governor." But he felt a coldness down his back. Carol Hardman had turned full circle on one thing. Yet he couldn't imagine . . . He could imagine it of Juliet. "I was in the bedroom with her, governor, before I knew I was, any damage was done before I began to talk." This was true, although he hadn't thought of it until now. Until the chief, with his objective view . . . The view he would have had, if he hadn't given his name and rank in a bar.

"I suppose so, Neil. You've done quite well. I knew I was right to suggest you had a look round."

Neil wondered which of the two of them the chief was feeling prouder of. It didn't matter, though. And underneath, he was sure, the chief always knew the real score.

"How did you persuade her to go with you, Neil?"

"I didn't. I tried, of course, and when she overreacted I left it while we talked about other things. Then suddenly she said she thought she would let me take her home after all. I can't deny I'd put forward some pretty cogent arguments in favour of it. There's just one more thing, governor. When the news goes out that Carol Hardman's come to light—as it'll have to do during the day— could you suppress the where and the how of her reappearance? I'm finished here otherwise." The chief grunted. Neil suspected he hadn't thought of that particular small complication. "You can say she just decided to come in. An unspecified hiding place where she got homesick and hungry."

"All right, Neil, we know what to say."

"Thank you, governor. I'll go now. Should make Southampton by ten. We'll be staying at the college until after breakfast tomorrow, by the way. Then back at The Fallow Deer."

"The Fallow Deer, yes. Look after that wife of yours."

"Will do, governor."

And Cathy would look after him. But he would not tell the chief that he had an unofficial colleague. The chief believed in women in their place. Even policewomen, which gave regular rise to bruised relations.

The view from the staircase now was quite different, the lights and shades more sharply differentiated, a green tinge entering the silver grass. The earlier cloud was breaking up into Impressionist dots against a pale blue sky. It was going to be a nice day. At least, driving to Southampton, he would see more of the morning than was visible through net curtain.

He had his report on tape, and in his mac pocket, before they went down to breakfast. He was actually telling Bertha Hazell, as they leaned towards one another across the space between their tables, how much he was looking forward to the morning session when he was summoned to the telephone.

Bob Ryan said, "I gather *rhubarb* would do?"

"Yes, only say it a few times will you, Bob. Are you coming?"

"Yes. With Sergeant Dobie and the father. You know how to get to Southampton HQ?"

"I've been there before, but remind me."

It would have been more painful for Cathy to compose her features to the expression of anguished disappointment which the supposed situation merited, but probably easier. He hoped he wasn't overdoing it.

"I just tempted fate," he lamented to Bertha Hazell as he paused by her chair. He noted that without the mask of her professional animation she looked ill. "There are two keys to a rather important cupboard in my office. One's been lost, and I've got the other."

"Oh, but surely"—Mrs. Hazell's immediate reaction, as of a

child deprived of a promised treat, made him realize she had enjoyed impressing him—"Can't they wait?"

"They're coming to Southampton. I'll only miss the morning, Bertha." The enormity of his deception of her made it difficult for him to use her first name.

"You needn't miss *anything?*" She beamed from him to Cathy and he saw how strong she was. To his contemptuous amusement he could feel himself actually tensing his bodily muscles against any sensible suggestion she was going to make. "One of our gardeners is going into Southampton this morning. He can take your key and you needn't—"

"I'm awfully afraid not, Bertha. It does sound ridiculous, but I'm just not allowed to entrust this particular key to anyone but the colleague who'll be coming for it." She had still not given up, and he leaned towards her, lowering his voice. "And if that sounds rather mysterious, I'll let it stand."

"Say no more, Neil." He had caught her imagination; he could see in her expressive face intrigued acceptance of an esoteric higher power.

"Bless you." By hinting that he was not quite what he seemed, he felt illogically eased in his conscience. "I don't deny it's an awful bore. I'll go now and hope to be back before the morning session's over." It was ten past nine and Carol would be on her way. Thank goodness it was a fine morning; he was quite sorry enough for her as it was.

Upstairs, Cathy said, "I'm glad Bertha thinks, now, that there's *something* funny about you; it makes me feel a tiny bit less of a hypocrite."

"I feel the same. Enjoy the morning, darling, you haven't any more work to do for me, you've already got under the guard of our key suspects. I don't mean suspects, of course," he said quickly, encountering her basilisk stare. "You know what I do mean."

"I hope so, Neil." He let her look chasten him, and then she said, smiling, "I haven't got anywhere with Hiatus Henry, nor will I."

"No. Even you. But—forgive me, darling, I must say it—

there's not the slightest possibility he could have been in London at the significant time."

He left her looking thoughtfully out of the window, and reached the designated lay-by just before half past nine. He would have liked to get out of the car but waited inside with his window down. It was only when he arrived that he began to worry that Carol might have changed her mind, to be angry with himself at what he all at once saw as a naivety in imagining she could not swing as abruptly away from her decision as she had swung towards it. But he had scarcely more than a minute of the new anxiety. Carol was scrambling into the car before he saw her leave the trees.

"No wife, Detective Inspector Carter? I think you made her up."

"My wife's listening to Mrs. Hazell talking about English furniture. I had to make an excuse to get away, if you think about it. Not necessary to make one for my wife as well."

"I thought you might feel safer with a chaperone."

"I survived last night." It was only by glancing at her that he remembered he was talking to a schoolgirl. She looked very young, her freckled face shining, her hair untidy and needing a wash. He wondered if she had been risking the bathroom or had made do with the tap of drinking water in the attic, but didn't ask her in case she thought he was implying that she smelt. She didn't, except faintly of scent. He noticed the shoulder bag, touched it.

"That was all you had?"

"Yes. I'd left my case in the flat. I wish I didn't have to go back to the flat."

"It'll be different now."

"It won't. Thanks for not saying anything."

"I promised I wouldn't. Thanks for turning up."

Having to look at the road, rather than at the girl, enabled them to continue their conversation almost as directly as the darkness had made possible.

"I was getting claustrophobia. And"—he felt her steal a glance at him—"I thought I'd like to see Mummy and Daddy."

"Your father's coming to Southampton with my colleague Detective Inspector Ryan."

Even above the engine he heard the sharp intake of breath. "How— how is he?"

"I don't know. I don't know any more than you do."

"Didn't you see him, then?"

"Yes, I did. But remember that was more than a week ago, and a week's a long time when you're almost out of your mind."

"Is he . . . Is Mummy . . ."

"*No*. And I shouldn't start worrying about that now."

"I'm sorry," she said humbly. "I know I've been awful."

"You have. I'm glad you know it. Is it good to be away from Bellfield House?"

"Yes, oh yes."

But she was in tears again. They lasted all the way to Southampton, although he had an idea she was rallying them in the last ten minutes.

When she got out of the car at headquarters, she looked up and down the street and he had a dreadful fancy she was going to bolt again. But she waited docilely enough as he came round and took her by the arm.

Bob Ryan was pacing about just inside, and Neil handed him the tape before greeting Carol's father in the small room which had been set aside for the reunion. He was aware of hostility mingling with the gratitude, but the poor blighter now would feel wary of any man he knew had been alone with his daughter. He was glad to see, as he turned to the door, Carol flinging herself into her father's arms, and being held there.

"You're the dark horse." Outside, Bob stared at him. Hostility again. "But of course, you weren't happy, were you? Is that why you booked a busman's honeymoon?"

Bob had been one of the team who'd been sent to Bellfield originally and had gone reluctantly, feeling London was the place to be. So it wasn't jealousy, so much as having been kept in the dark about something and nothing. It was a bit of a pity—Neil hadn't imagined Bob, or any of them, ever needing to be told. He hadn't worried at any point that the chief might tell. Until now, of course. Now that Neil had come up with something. At any rate, with someone.

"It was exactly that, Bob. And I didn't want to be laughed at any more, you gave me enough stick for going on the usual sort of honeymoon."

"The chief didn't tell me much." Bob, appeased, was looking at him beseechingly.

"It was the most extraordinary luck. Play the tape on the way back. I'm still crazy, but there are one or two interesting things. What about Tate?"

"Nothing. Still protesting his innocence. Getting a bit desperate, actually. His lawyer's asked us to lay off a bit."

"What he says all fits with finding the girl was under age."

"I know, Neil, I know."

"There's no way we can find anything more than circumstantial evidence. And even that . . . His dabs were all over the place anyway, for God's sake."

"D'you have another suspect, Neil?"

Cathy's face rose warningly in front of him. "No. Oh no." And anyway, he didn't.

"You're just not happy?"

"Are you?"

Bob shrugged. As he himself would no doubt have done, if he hadn't brought about his special connection with the case of Juliet Payne.

"Anyway," said Neil. "I *am* happy, as a matter of fact. I'm having a wonderful time."

"But you'll stay for a coffee?"

Absurdly he hesitated before accepting, because of delaying his return to Cathy without being taken nearer to the truth of Juliet. He missed the coffee break at Bellfield House and crept into the second lecture room just as his conscientious wife was asking the tutor a question. Not her first; she'd done her stuff the day before and opened a minor floodgate.

There was a seat for him at the end of a row, next to her. She was asking something about the difference between real Chinese lacquer and European imitative japanning, she and Mrs. Hazell were bandying words such as "whiting," "mastic," "gum arabic." What hidden knowledge had *he* with which to surprise and delight (or perhaps intimidate) *her?* None, he thought, and would have felt naked and ashamed if he had not remembered that she loved him. Admired him too, which for all his seeming confidence was the fact about her which astonished him most.

During lunch he realized that some tension had gone out of him. Perhaps, despite what Bob Ryan had said about Frank Tate continuing to plead his innocence, he was becoming reconciled to the unsatisfactory idea that the surface of things was the truth of them. Anyway, he couldn't really imagine anyone in Bellfield having been responsible for Juliet Payne's death. What was he looking for?

Only something to explain those few words of hers and the aura of innocence which persisted in hanging about the figure of Frank Tate.

Pretty feeble stuff.

And he was afraid that he might also be looking for a new role for himself to offset the first one. He'd rather think that he wanted some clues about Juliet, about how and why the child had turned into the girl. Which of course he did. Although there was nothing he could do with them when he got them, except feel more depressingly involved.

Would he have felt as he did if he hadn't got Cathy; was he perhaps trying to earn his undeserved happiness? He had always had an uncomfortable sense of right and wrong, even when he disregarded it.

Lunch was a merry meal. The course had reached the stage of seeming to have been going on forever, while becoming more precious by reason of its end being almost in sight. Cathy seemed to know everyone on it, and even he was differentiating between one or two of them. Any restraint between tutor and students was quite broken down, and Bertha Hazell was now constantly surrounded. Neil thought nearly all her class were in the group which left the dining room via the main lecture room, in order to be amused by the sight of the black-and-white cat relaxing across the centre of the floor.

In the hall Neil took Cathy's hand.

"Don't let's go upstairs, let's go into the garden. D'you know, you've stopped me enjoying myself alone in the car?"

"I'm sorry, Neil."

"So am I, in a way, it was always something . . . Let's go right down to the bottom."

The donkey was there, resting its grey plush neck on the old wall which divided the grounds of Bellfield House from the heath. Looking back at the house, Neil thought he could pick out Juliet's small window.

"I can feel her out here," he said, "more than I can in the house."

"She must have played here; it's a marvellous garden for a child."

"She and Carol, getting an appetite up for the nighttime. Cathy . . ."

She took her hand from the donkey's neck and it jutted its head crossly into her side. "Let's look round. I know it's silly, but . . ."

They found it quite quickly, in a corner, in among the trees. An amateur job, but looking unmistakably a miniature house. There were even the remains of a miniature garden in the clearing in front of it, marked out with seashells. The door and the one windowsill had once been painted yellow. Neil looked at his watch as he found the door was unlocked.

"We've got ten minutes."

Inside, there were two cane chairs, each with a faded red cushion, a wicker table carrying two or three magazines for teenagers, a cupboard which looked as if it had come out of a maid's bedroom of the thirties.

In the poor light the cupboard seemed to be bare, but when he moved his hand about, it encountered one or two small things. A stub of lipstick. A tub of red powder with a piece of stained cotton wool. A bottle with some inky fluid Cathy said was eyeliner. A handbag mirror with rouged smudges, which he wrapped in his handkerchief and put carefully into his pocket.

"Beginnings?"

"Would your colleagues have come down here?"

"I don't know. Nothing was said about it."

He got down on his knees on the edge of the worn brown carpet and felt carefully along every part of the two shelves, finding only a splinter, which was long enough for him easily to pull out. He moved his hand up and down the inner sides more carefully, but even so the sudden sharp edge of folded paper cut the soft pad of his fingertip. As he sucked it, he asked Cathy to ease the paper out, put it on the table and open it.

It looked like some sort of handwritten draft—three blue ballpoint paragraphs, with frequent crossings out.

"Is it her writing, Neil?"

"I don't know. It's absurd, I don't know."

"Will you take it?"

"Yes. We'll read it upstairs."

The paper, too, he folded into his handkerchief.

Outside, under the window, was an oblong of cardboard. Neil kicked it gently over. KEEP OUT was written in large uneven red capitals.

"Juliet's kingdom," said Cathy tremulously. "Don't you think so?"

"I do, yes."

They went back up the garden quickly, not just because time was short. He knew Cathy had found the atmosphere in that small bare room as disheartening as it had been for him. Bertha Hazell was well into her stride before the two objects he was now carrying ceased to burn his body.

At teatime Peter Cowley came over and stood beside them. Neil thought a lasting improvement in his appearance had resulted from his tête-à-tête with Cathy the day before, but he was still ill at ease. Which, of course, he might always have been. It was a monstrous disadvantage, in his trade, not to know what people had been like before a murder.

"We had a look round the garden at lunchtime," said Neil to Cowley. "Came across a little house right at the bottom."

Cowley's rather prominent adam's apple shot sharply up his throat, and his features looked suddenly vague, almost lopsided. His problem, now, was to withhold his tears.

Bertha said softly, "It was Juliet's little den."

"I'm sorry," said Cathy. "If we'd realized . . ."

"It's all right, how could you know. And anyway," said Bertha determinedly, "we mustn't try to avoid speaking about her."

"She spent a lot of time in the little house?"

"Oh, when she was smaller. Not so much . . . lately. I'm sure it must be awfully dilapidated, I haven't been down there for months."

"It's . . ." They all turned towards Peter Cowley, but he seemed unable to say any more.

"I don't think I'd like to *live* with Rococo furniture, would any of you?" Cathy looked from one to another of the nearest members of the English furniture course, who had been politely disguising their attention. "It's very elegant but it doesn't invite you to relax."

"I think you may covet some of the small Sheraton pieces I'm going to show you." Bertha Hazell smiled gratefully at Cathy, and Neil saw the frown between his wife's brows. When would the return of Carol Hardman be made public? He thought he honestly felt as troubled by his deception as by the ever-present danger of being discovered. Which until recently would not have been the case. There was no doubt allying himself with Cathy had made a change in his perceptions.

Back in the second lecture room, Bertha showed them a slide of a lady's rosewood writing desk of the late-eighteenth century, then unveiled the desk itself as her culminating treasure. She finished the course by sitting down on her Regency dining chair while her students applauded. Neil saw the animation fade from her face in the few seconds it took for the applause to die away. But she was smiling again as she reminded them about the after-dinner quiz.

"Businesslike," she said, "with written answers, which I shall mark. I'll announce the winner at breakfast before you go your separate ways, and I've a little prize. Not one of these things, I'm afraid."

Neil and Cathy were going to read the sheet of paper as soon as they got upstairs, but as they unlocked their door they became so aware of one another they only just had time to get down to the bar without once again being later than everyone else. They were greeted warmly on every side, but the atmosphere seemed slightly less festive and carefree. A sense of imminent departure? Neil fancied one or two of the older, unaccompanied members of the courses were already aware of the coming morning, with its end to this hothouse growth of civilized companionship. From warm to cold. From light to dark. Like Juliet . . .

Another, more immediate and brutal, reality had broken in on Bertha Hazell. She came into the bar just before dinner was announced, and Neil knew that she had heard about Carol.

"What is it?" He had ordered the dry martini he knew was her usual drink and he put it into her hand.

"Juliet's friend Carol's turned up. I heard it on the news and perhaps that's why it shook me. If the police had got in touch, I'd have had a moment to get ready."

Cathy passed her hand across her face.

"Yes," said Neil. "Do you want to tell us?"

Bertha drained her drink. "There's nothing to tell, they didn't really say anything. Just that she'd been hiding and had decided to give herself up. I don't mean that, of course, she hadn't done anything wrong." For the second time, Neil saw the generous mouth draw in. "That is, she didn't kill Juliet, of course, but there are other things . . . I shall want to see her."

"Of course you will," said Neil on a lurch of dismay. He hadn't thought of the inevitable get-together of Bertha and Carol, but of course he had had no thoughts, before last night, so far as Carol was concerned. At least she wouldn't share Bertha's eagerness for a meeting; she would make excuses for a day or so. Perhaps until he and Cathy had left Bellfield . . .

"Little tart," said Bertha. There was no doubt that Carol Hardman had been of real help to her in her efforts to accept the fact of Marilyn.

"She was very wrong to hide from her parents," said Cathy. "Did you dislike her when she used to come here?"

"No," said Bertha reluctantly. "No, I didn't. I thought she was a not very bright but quite pleasant sort of a girl. As a matter of fact, I always thought it was Juliet who had the ideas and was the leader. It just shows how you can be deceived."

"Yes, indeed." Neil couldn't believe that self-deception was part of this strong woman's nature in the ordinary way, but he hoped circumstances would allow her to go on hiding behind this particular piece of it.

By the time the quiz began, she had either absorbed the news or laid it aside. She was at her liveliest, infecting her students as all through the course with her enthusiasm. After a laughter-punctuated but on the whole serious couple of hours, Neil was about to ask her if in view of his morning absence he could be excused from handing in his paper, when Miss Booth appeared beside him and told him he was wanted on the telephone. If he would take the call in her office . . .

He hadn't yet caught Bertha's attention and he sidled out of the room. Miss Booth was already back at her desk, holding the telephone receiver out to him with an efficient smile.

"Thank you, Miss Booth."

She hesitated only briefly. "When you've finished, Mr. Carter, if you'd just close the door."

"Of course. I hope I'm not—"

"I have duties elsewhere."

He waited the long moment while she crossed to the door, shut it behind her.

"Hello?"

"Neil." As always, the chief failed to identify himself, but the one word, as always, was sufficient. "Can you talk?"

"Apparently. But somebody could just be on the way to an extension."

"I'll tell you the gist of it and you can ring me back from that call box. Tate's alibi's turned up and we're having to release him in the morning. It's all wide open. You've got the choice of moving out of Bellfield as quietly as you moved in, or turning official. Ring me back, will you, in the next ten minutes."

CHAPTER 11

He was surprised to find that his first sensation was dismay. Wasn't this what he had been hoping for? He did not like his ridiculous feeling that he himself had been shaping events, to bring them to this point. But would his superiors be turning their attention so sharply to Bellfield if he hadn't repeated those words? *I can never get away from home, never, never, never . . .*

What to decide?

The chief had said ten minutes, and he spent five in the cloakroom next to the telephone kiosk. Things weren't any clearer when he came out.

The chief answered in person on the second ring.

"I'm staying this end," he said, as if their conversation had not been interrupted. "And we're starting to check statements." Neil had a sudden painful picture of the old music master. "Bob Ryan'll be coming down to Bellfield in the morning with a sergeant. I rather think the super has a mind to join them." The chief sighed. "I'm not trying to influence you, Neil. Any ill feeling generated by what might be called your deception could be counterproductive. On the other hand, if you've made any personal headway, you might just be the one to prepare the ground. Neil?"

"I'm here, governor." In the small round mirror on the wall of the kiosk, his face had an unhealthy look, but that could be the poor light.

"You'll have to tell me now. I wanted to give you the chance, but we've got to get on with things."

"I know." If he could just shut off his personal reactions.

"Well, then?"

On a rush of relief, he found that his inclinations coincided with his idea of where his continuing usefulness might lie. He did not wish to go through life parrying attempts by Bertha Hazell to be their friend. Far better for her never to make any.

"I'll stay, governor. I'll make myself known."

"Right you are." The chief didn't show whether or not he was pleased. "The brother and sister for the time being, I think."

"It's bedtime here, governor, can I wait till the morning? There won't be any press announcement tonight, will there, about Tate? That would give me time to get some sort of programme going."

"You won't have much time in the morning. Bob and company should be with you by ten."

"I'll manage. I'll get Payne and Mrs. Hazell together first thing."

"All right, Neil." The chief was making sure he sounded doubtful. "Bob and company will go straight to the college."

"I'll be waiting for them. What happened with Tate's alibi?"

"Abroad, we suspect unofficially. Tate's lawyer had a permanent call out for him, and he came panting in. It all checks."

"I see. So Tate's out."

"I should be more inclined to put it that other people are in. You'd better have something ready for Ryan and company in the morning. To say nothing of the super."

"Of course, governor."

At least the collection of the quiz papers had been made. Bertha Hazell shook her finger at him as he returned laggingly to his seat.

"Mr. Carter, did you arrange that interruption?"

He disguised the small shock with an effortful smile. The seated rows were breaking up and she came over to them. Tonight she was wearing a white frilled blouse and long dark skirt. Her personality was very strong.

"There's nothing I'd like this moment more than a last drink with you both, but I have to get home, I'm expecting a telephone call." Her grateful smile Neil knew was smiting them both. "Last drink, that was a silly thing to say. Quite apart from the fact that I may find myself drinking my breakfast coffee with you in the morning—yes, I'm breakfasting in college again—I shall surely see you at least once before you leave the forest. You said you were going back to The Fallow Deer in the morning?"

"Yes," said Neil glumly. He wondered how he had ever considered things difficult before the chief's call. Cathy said that she, too, was sure they would meet again.

He told her the moment the bedroom door was shut.

"You're sorry," she said, studying his face.

"Yes."

"I misjudged you. Perhaps you misjudged yourself. Do you have a feeling about anyone? I wouldn't ask you before, but I must now."

"No one. Oh, darling, I should have spoken to Bertha tonight. My chief won't be waiting for the morning." They put their arms round one another and he pushed his face into her hair. "I've got to have something fresh and useful for the team. Which could include the superintendent."

"You've already given them Carol Hardman. And you've been justified over Frank Tate. And that piece of paper might help. Let's read it."

The three paragraphs were without address, date, top, or tail, but they undoubtedly made up a letter or part of one. Under the bright ring of the table lamp, the blue ballpoint script was revealed to have a rather characterless clarity which Cathy greeted with amused recognition as being that most commonly found among the alumnae of girls' public and private schools.

"It's very like Winnie's writing and it's like the writing of half the girls I'm teaching at the moment."

"What sort of age?"

"Oh, teenage. If it's Juliet, I should think it's fairly recent."

He took her hands, partly to prevent her forgetting and touching the paper. They read against the voices of mature students on the landing outside their door, reiterating reluctant adieux.

I have received your letter and I accept your apology. Of course there is no reason why we should not be friends but what you did was not friendship and upset me very much.

I am too young to be more than a friend to you, and if I know this you should know it too, you are older than I am and you should be more responsible.

I will not say anything to my father, but if you attempt to be more than friends with me again then I am afraid I will have to tell him. I know you like your work here, and will not want that to happen.

The crossings out made it difficult to read fluently, but the sense was plain. Neil welcomed his sharp sense of distaste; it was an antidote at last to his regret. Yet at the same time he had a curious feeling of disappointment, disillusionment even.

"Little bitch!" He had to make himself say it, and it didn't seem to do him any good. "Whichever role she took on, she played it to the full. Butter wouldn't melt in Miss Juliet Payne's mouth."

"We knew that already, didn't we?" Cathy crossed the room, kicked off her shoes and lay down on the bed, her hands behind her head. "I mean, that photograph."

"Yes. That poor little sod Cowley. Not that the letter was necessarily sent. But something gave rise to that draft." Carefully he folded the paper and put it in a college envelope from the little writing table. He took his shoes off too and went to lie beside Cathy. He wished he had the statements in front of him again, although he remembered them quite well. In one case, at least, they were possibly misleading.

"Cowley in his statement made no mention of being anywhere near the Knightsbridge flat. He could be lying, or Carol Hardman could have a grudge."

"She could be jealous that he fancied Juliet?"

"She hardly knew him. She could have been jealous of Juliet as Juliet. Her strength. Her strange sort of charisma." He had met Marilyn, but it was Juliet he knew. "Why should Juliet have a monopoly of stirring it? Carol could have asked that question. Could. *Could.*" Irritably he loosened his tie. "No one but Tate has faced any real questioning as yet. At least it should be comparatively simple to get at the truth about the people who weren't supposed to be in London that Sunday. It's always easier for people geographically near the scene of a crime to lie about their precise whereabouts. They're expected to have been in the neighbourhood at least, whereas if you've come a few hundred miles out of your way it's not so easy to fudge it unless you have phenomenal luck."

"Neil."

"What is it?" Something in her tone made him give her his full attention.

"Before you went off this morning, you said something about it being absolutely impossible for Henry Payne to have been in London at the time Juliet was killed."

"It is impossible."

"Oh, I'm sure, yes, but you saying that made me start thinking about things *looking* impossible but actually not being. I mean . . ." In her diffident enthusiasm she tossed over on to her side to lie gazing at him. There was a shine on the skin round her nose and in the centre of her pointed chin. He was so aware of the life in her he imagined warming his hands at it. The tenderness he knew was in his face still felt unfamiliar. "You told me Bertha Hazell had spent that Saturday night with a friend in Southampton and was back home by lunchtime. But if no one actually saw her, then she *could* have gone on to London and . . . and . . . Whatever happened between her and Juliet, she could have got back much later and just *said* she was home by lunchtime. If she was seen arriving at her house say at four o'clock, she could have said she'd been out for a run or something."

He felt the dismay again, although of course this was basic stuff and he'd have to have considered it sooner or later. "She could, but what made you start working all that out? You didn't approve of my speculations?"

She looked apologetic. "I didn't start to work it out, it just came into my head as a sort of general idea—the idea that perhaps we're ready to believe things which sound likely and reasonable without really examining them." She stopped. Her eyes were enormous. "Oh Neil, how awful, I forgot for a moment I was talking to a policeman. Of course, you're *trained*—"

"We're supposed to be."

"I only mentioned Bertha Hazell because of her being so unlikely. Poor Peter Cowley seems more likely. But there's cold fish John Hazell. And there's even Miss Booth, I suppose, if no one saw her on Sunday morning. And other men like Frank Tate . . . I wonder if your super would be thinking of coming to Bellfield if you hadn't kept on at your chief?"

His own uncomfortable question. "I wonder."

"It's awful, but it does look a bit bad, doesn't it, for Peter Cowley? I mean, there's that letter now . . ."

"I know."

Cowley. An aura of innocence far stronger than that surrounding Frank Tate. Perhaps unnaturally strong . . . If only that wretched well-fed, luxuriously uniformed hall porter had come on at twelve instead of one. But the empty desk didn't have to have been the murderer's luck, it could have been his or her reward for good planning . . .

The freeing of Frank Tate, justifying his own unofficial investigations, might make it a little easier to disillusion Bertha Hazell.

Not easy enough, though, to give him much prospect of sleep. He sat up and looked at the clock.

"Are you going to get undressed, Neil?"

The question was maternal, rather than erotic. He could see in her face that she was concerned for him. In her presence he was inclined to give his emotions the facial expression he gave them when he was alone. It was one of the marvellous things about her, that he should find himself doing that. And she would not think of it as being hard on her.

"No. It's only eleven. I'm going to see Bertha Hazell now and tell her the score. It ought to be Payne first, as the father, but I'd rather start with Bertha. It'll give her a chance to brace herself for the others"—he would always feel uncomfortable at not having prepared her for the reappearance of Carol Hardman, even though there had been no way he could have done it—"and for me it's the only chance of an eventual night's sleep."

Her smile was wonderful.

"I'm so glad, Neil, I'm sure it'll make it a bit easier for her."

"I want you to come with me. Just to be there in a sort of WPC role. She'll be less likely to think I'm mad, or try to call the police." They grinned at one another. "I shan't want you to say anything."

"I wouldn't!"

"I'm sorry, I know you wouldn't. But I do really think it would be a good thing."

"Then I'll come, of course."

They had only to put on their shoes and their jackets. Perhaps they had kept the rest of their clothes on because of a subconscious suspicion that they would in the end seek out Bertha Hazell before morning.

The bar had only just closed and there were still people in the hall—two couples Cathy said belonged to Stress, the wives with diaries in their hands. An open door revealed a bridge four still at table.

The barman, questioned through his grille, assured them the front door was never locked before midnight, if they fancied a stroll.

If they were with Bertha Hazell beyond that time, she would have a key.

Despite the uneasiness which rippled between them, they both paused on the forecourt, at the beauty of the night. The sky was high and clear, the silver moon tinted gold and dull enough for them to see the pattern of the stars which gave velvet texture to the inky dark. An owl hooted softly, there was a mouselike shriek of fear or pain. He would rather have walked hand in hand and in silence than start the car into that layered stillness, but they must use what time they had.

The space outside the two garages opposite the cottages was empty and he swung onto it, aware of the lighted window beside Bertha Hazell's front door. He wasn't working out what he would say to her; that would be determined by her reception of them, by what he could only ever call, in his habitual pragmatic way, the influences of the moment.

A light snapped on over the porch as the door was opened. His finger was still on the bell. She would have seen them through her spy hole, anxious and close together.

"Forgive us. It's rather important."

"What can have happened since we said good night?" She beamed on them. Neil thought that even after her arduous day she saw them as a welcome extension of reprieve from her thoughts.

"Come in, come in." Touching each other's fingertips, they followed her into her sitting room. She had been sitting under the one lighted lamp, reading. He saw a picture of an old chair in the open book and felt a pang of pity. "You'll have a drink now, you must."

"No!" Neil's vehemence arrested her as she crossed the room, and she turned back to them. "Not yet, anyway," he amended more gently. "Bertha . . ."

"It *is* important. I can see. Sit down."

He knew as they slowly grouped themselves in a small circle that he was going to begin by telling her about Tate's release. Probably for his own good, doing it that way could only distract her full attention from his subsequent revelation that he had so carefully deceived her. But possibly for hers as well: the Tate blow would be as bad delivered first or second; the other one perhaps less so, in a suddenly more dangerous world.

"Well?" she said. She was looking only at him, but he glanced at Cathy, making herself narrow in a generous chair, her head down between her hunched shoulders and her hands plunged between her knees. It was an odd moment in which to realize how much one loved one's wife.

"Frank Tate," he said, turning back to Bertha. "His alibi's turned up and the police have had to let him go. He couldn't have murdered Juliet."

"Couldn't have . . ." He didn't think he had ever seen health fade so swiftly from a face. Cathy was across the room, her arm round the drooping shoulders as Bertha swayed forward. Neil was on his feet and walking the way Bertha Hazell had been walking so strongly the moment before. He found brandy in the corner cupboard and poured a small measure.

"Drink this."

Cathy took the glass from him and held it to Bertha's lips. She drank a little, coughed, and pulled herself upright, colour returning blotchily to her face.

"I've just heard the radio news. There wasn't anything . . ." He saw hostility in her eyes. "How could you know anything about Tate . . . about Juliet . . . I don't believe you." She tried to draw away from Cathy. The hostility was being edged out of her face by fear, dawning realization that it was two to one.

He said quickly, "I'm a police officer, Bertha, that's how I know, that's why you have to believe me. I'm Detective Inspector Neil Carter of Scotland Yard." Would he ever again announce himself without wincing inside? "I actually arrested Frank Tate for the murder of your niece." He would not tell her yet the circumstances in which he had done that. Not, he thought, that she would take it in, she didn't seem to be taking in anything beyond his first revelation of Tate's innocence. The fear had faded from her eyes, leaving them blank. "Even though all the evidence seemed to point to Tate, I somehow wasn't satisfied and I decided to come down to Bellfield with Cathy after our wedding on Saturday and just try and get to know something about Juliet's background and family." Even his supplementary revelation that Cathy was a bride failed to produce a reaction; she continued to stare at him expressionlessly. He found it unnerving. "I'm afraid I deceived you, Bertha, but it was for Juliet's sake."

"For Juliet's sake." The words came like a faint echo.

"I wanted to make sure that justice would be done, Bertha." He leaned towards her, looking at Cathy kneeling beside her, rather than at those unseeing eyes. "The case is open again, the police are coming back to Bellfield. I've been put in charge on the spot, and two of my colleagues will be here in the morning. Maybe my superintendent. This time, unless they find the murderer in London, they'll be checking up on the statements everyone made. Peter Cowley, Miss Booth, yourself. Your brother is the only person from Bellfield who couldn't have been in London that Sunday morning. Peter Cowley was, Miss Booth could have been, all we can be sure of at the moment is that she wasn't at the college. Even you, Bertha, could have gone on to London from Southampton and arrived back in Bellfield later than the time you told us you arrived back. Forgive me, of course I'm not suggesting that that's what you did, I'm only pointing out that if no one saw you here in Bellfield before late afternoon it *is* technically possible for you to have been in London and you will be subject to the questioning which—"

"What did you just say?"

He could barely hear her. Cathy ventured to lean up and replace her arm round Bertha's shoulders. She seemed unaware of the renewed contact.

"I said that now Frank Tate has had to be released, everyone else who could possibly have been in London at the time—"

"About me. What did you say about me?"

"I said the police would have to check up on whether you really did come straight back to Bellfield from Southampton or whether you in fact went to London first and then came home. But of course I was only trying to prepare you for the kind of situation—"

"The police would have to do that?"

"Well, yes. You see—"

"You mean they would actually consider that I might have killed Juliet?"

"They have to consider every possibility." He caught Cathy's eye and she made an apologetic grimace. "And it is just a possibility. Forgive me, Bertha, I—"

"Then, I must tell them."

"Tell *me*, Bertha. Tell me what?"

She stared through him. "That I did kill Juliet. That I did go on to London from Southampton and get home in the late afternoon." It was as if she was repeating something she knew by heart. Cathy drew back from the suddenly square shoulders.

"Mrs. Hazell"—he had reverted to formality on a reflex, before he realized that from now on it would have to be Mrs. Hazell—"before you say anything more I must remind you of what I have just said. That I'm a police officer in the Metropolitan Force and that I've been put in charge of the Bellfield end of the investigation into Juliet Payne's death."

"Yes," she said impatiently. "That's why I'm telling you. That I killed her. I can't let anyone else suffer for what I did."

"Frank Tate could have suffered." He hadn't meant to be deflected, he hadn't begun to make a moral judgment, his oblique admonishment was another reflex.

"I know," she said. "I think . . . I would have spoken eventually even if . . . I wouldn't have let him take the blame. I was trying to get my courage up, but now . . . I'd rather tell the police than be found out."

"Well, you've done that." He said slowly and clearly, "I'm not a civil servant, Mrs. Hazell, I'm a policeman. Please accept my personal apologies for our deception. It was in the cause of the truth."

"The truth," said Mrs. Hazell, suddenly decisive. "You've got the truth now." She stood up, jutting her chin. He could imagine her as head girl at school, at attention during assembly. "I left Peggy in Southampton at ten, as I said I did, but I didn't come straight home, I went on to London, to the Hardmans' flat, to see Juliet."

"But why didn't you tell your friend you were going to do that? Had you decided then to . . . kill Juliet?"

"No!" She flinched, sat down again. "But Peggy knows I was worried about her, I told her I was worried. I wanted to see Juliet in London with— with Carol and Carol's parents. I thought it might give me some kind of a clue about her, about why she'd been so strange . . ." For a few seconds he thought she might faint, but she rallied. "If it didn't, I thought of going to see her music teacher . . . But I hadn't really made up my mind to go to London at all, even when I turned out of Peggy's gate I wasn't sure . . . And if I had been, I wouldn't have wanted Peggy to know what a silly, unnecessary thing I was going to do. You said you were the police, Mr. Carter, why aren't you writing it down?"

"Because I wasn't expecting it and I haven't got a junior officer." He managed to smile at her, but she didn't notice. Any more than she had noticed anything so trivial as a couple of strangers telling her lies about themselves.

"Oh, if that's the trouble . . ." She got up again and crossed the room in her usual decisive way, noisily unearthed a tape recorder from a cupboard, set it sharply on the table beside her chair and flicked switches. "There we are."

"Thank you," said Neil, "that's very helpful."

"I'll begin again." Talking loudly and almost aggressively, Bertha Hazell told the machine that she had driven to London on the spur of the moment after leaving her friend in Southampton.

"Where did you park?"

"Park?" She looked startled. "Down a side street. By the flats, I think, I was so het up with myself I hardly noticed . . . Yes," she said firmly, "it was by the flats. Sunday. Yellow lines not operating. Not that I noticed."

"Did you see anyone, Mrs. Hazell? Outside, or in the public parts of the building?"

She stared. "Of course there were people outside the building. I can't remember them."

"No one you knew?"

"Certainly no one I knew."

With a pettish gesture she wrenched table and tape recorder forward so that they stood between her and Neil.

"No one you knew inside the building, either? When you arrived, and . . . when you left?"

"I didn't see anyone I knew anywhere in London that day."

"What happened when you arrived, Mrs. Hazell?"

"I went upstairs," she said, staring through him again. "And I rang the bell and Juliet answered it." Twelve noon or thereabouts? She would have thought it was him. Or the someone she was expecting? "Only, I didn't realize for a moment that it was Juliet. She saw that I hadn't recognized her, she started to close the door on me, but suddenly I could see . . ." Bertha Hazell dropped her head on her breast.

"I shall have to ring my office," said Neil gently and carefully, "and ask my colleagues to come. You must go back to London with them tonight, as you'll appreciate. I'd like to use your telephone now and I suggest you and my wife go into the kitchen and make some tea or coffee."

She raised her head. "I haven't finished telling you."

"I know. We'll carry on as soon as I've rung my chief."

He forgot to hope that Mrs. Larkin wouldn't answer his call. When she did, the absolute necessity of his getting hold of her husband seemed to communicate itself to her without the usual wordplay. The chief told Neil he had been in his first sleep.

"I'm sorry, governor. This seems to be revelation week. I decided I'd follow Mrs. Hazell home and tell her the situation tonight. She's confessed to the murder." The chief didn't even grunt. "Actually set up the tape recorder so that she can tell me all about it."

"Neil, I know this is the first of April, but a joke is a joke." The chief's voice was comparatively weak.

"I'd forgotten it was the first of April—actually, the thirty-first of March still has five minutes to go—but I'm afraid I'm not joking. The lady protests a great deal, but it could all be as she says."

"Could?"

"Disregard that, it's just that nothing seems to satisfy me these days. Except my marriage, of course. Governor, can you organize a couple to come up here right away now and take her back to town? We'll go on recording while she's so much in the mood, and they can take the tape back with them. We're at Ivy Cottage, as I think I said. I brought my wife with me, as there wasn't a convenient WPC. We'll stay with Mrs. Hazell here of course until the contingent arrives."

"Of course. You can talk to Payne and the other college people in the morning." The chief spoke as if he was offering a concession, but Neil hadn't got round to realizing he would have to talk to them at all. His reluctance was a cold rod replacing his spine. "Better present yourself at the local station, too."

"Yes, governor. Can you send a man to be here about the time in the morning Bob and company were originally coming, so that we can take further statements? Would it be too much to ask for David Hughes?"

The chief grunted.

"Whoever it is can take the statements back to London, and I can go back to The Fallow Deer and resume my honeymoon."

It wasn't so much that at this exact moment resuming his honeymoon was what he most wanted to do, it was more that he had got used to asserting his rights on those rare occasions where the opportunity offered.

"Of course, Neil," agreed the chief expansively. "I'll try to get the first contingent to you within three hours or so. Record all you can."

"Mrs. Hazell will see to that, unless her mood changes."

The only change, when he went back into the sitting room and Cathy poured each of them a cup of tea, was that Bertha Hazell seemed less aggressive. She told him the shock of recognizing Juliet had been severe, and Juliet had poured her a glass of brandy. Juliet had then tried to tell her she had just been dressing up, but Bertha had sensed the truth. When accused, Juliet had ceased to be conciliatory, had become defiant.

"She rammed her behaviour down my throat. She taunted me with it. She made me feel old and stupid. She said she hadn't started yet, what she'd done so far was nothing. I couldn't listen to any more of it, I ran at her, and she ran away from me, laughing. She ran into the bedroom and I followed her. The bed was all rumpled, sordid, horrible. She threw herself on it, still laughing. The tights were on the bed and I picked them up and got them round her neck—I'm strong and she's—she was small and slight, oh God, I pulled her towards me by the tights, I knotted the feet of them, I pulled and pulled. I didn't want to kill her, I wanted to stop her laughing, stop her being so pleased with the dreadful things she was doing . . . Doing to herself . . . Oh God, she died without a chance to repent, she died in her sins. Because I killed her."

Bertha Hazell sobbed heavily into her lap, Cathy's arms again around her. So the circumstances of Juliet's death had for her self-confessed killer a theological dimension. If Bertha Hazell believed she had destroyed her niece's soul as well as her body, the weight on her would have been crushing. All the more remarkable her fortitude in the last few days.

"Then you left?" prompted Neil after a short pause in which the sobs began to diminish.

"I left then. Yes."

"By the lift? Had you gone up in the lift?"

She stared again, starting the germ of an idea far down in his mind.

"I left by the stairs. I couldn't have waited for the lift. I had to run. I went up in the lift."

"You came straight home then? You didn't visit Juliet's music master?"

"No, no. I was in too much of a panic, I just wanted to get home."

"Yes, of course. You would be in too much of a panic to think about fingerprints."

Bertha Hazell reached out for her tea and took hold of the elegant cup, cradling it in her hands. "I was in a panic, but I did think about fingerprints. I wiped the glass and the doors where I'd touched them or thought I might have done. I hadn't touched anything in the bedroom except . . . I didn't think there would be any fingerprints in the bedroom."

"I see. Tell me just one thing more now, Mrs. Hazell. Did you tell Juliet you were coming to London to see her?"

She looked puzzled. "Tell Juliet? Of course I didn't. I've just said, I only decided on the spur of the moment, and the whole point was to catch her unawares. Oh God—"

"Did Juliet tell you she was expecting someone?"

He saw the horror in her eyes, turning to fear. "She didn't tell me." She spoke so softly he had to lean forward. "But she must have been. She must have . . . dressed up like that." She raised her head and her voice. "Someone had been there earlier. The bed . . ."

"We'll leave it there, Mrs. Hazell, and my wife will go upstairs with you to help you put a few things into a case. Then the three of us will rest down here until my colleagues arrive."

"So that's all?" On her feet, she stood very straight.

"For the time being." He thought she had had enough. And he wouldn't tell her now that it was he who had found Juliet's body. Anyway, that fact had become irrelevant. And, if she didn't know, the germ of his idea could have a better chance of growing . . .

Cathy dozed off a couple of times while they waited, but he and Bertha Hazell sat staring round them, occasionally meeting each other's eyes and looking away without acknowledgment. He took her key to the front door of Bellfield House, and he and Cathy were in bed just before four.

He was almost asleep when he heard her voice, soft but determined.

"Neil, d'you feel happier now, d'you feel you've got at the truth?"

"Oh darling, I don't really feel any different." He had answered without thinking what he was going to say.

CHAPTER 12

At half past eight he knocked on the door marked PRINCIPAL, hardly expecting or desiring a response, but realizing it would be a good thing if he could tell the Introduction to English Furniture course that Mrs. Hazell wasn't at breakfast because he had heard from somewhere or other that she was ill. If he didn't get the chance to tell Henry Payne she wouldn't be at breakfast because she had confessed to the murder of his daughter, then obviously he couldn't venture to explain her absence to his fellow students and would have to appear as puzzled as they were, a piece of playacting he could well do without.

So he was relieved rather than not when the quiet voice told him to come in.

Henry Payne was sitting behind his desk in an untidy surround of books and papers, looking as if he had been immersed in them for hours. Perhaps he had—Neil could imagine that this office might be the scholar's one place of intermittent solace.

"What can I do for you, Mr. Carter?" The smile was gently inquiring.

He had not expected the principal of Bellfield House to remember his name, and for a wildly hopeful moment he wondered if the chief had been extraordinarily kind to him.

"Dr. Payne, have you heard in the last few hours from the Metropolitan Police?"

He was barely through the question when he realized how absurd it was.

"No. Why do you ask?" But the polite face was scarcely interested. Payne had probably remembered his name because some private Pelmanism had happened to work.

"Because I told your sister last night that I am a police officer from Scotland Yard—detective inspector—and she then informed me that it was she who killed your daughter." There was no way of wrapping up information so uncompromisingly unpleasant. He noted his sudden formal phraseology. "Two of my colleagues came down from London and she went back with them." There was no emotion in the face before him. It could be, of course, that Dr. Payne was wondering how to deal safely and tactfully with a madman. He laid his ID on the desk.

"Oh, I believe you, Inspector Carter. Although I am puzzled that you pretended to be a civil servant."

Could it be that Henry Payne was detached enough actually to have decided to take the smaller problem first?

"Because I—as opposed to my colleagues—wasn't happy about the arrest of Frank Tate and thought I would use a week's leave to come down here and take a look at Juliet's background. You'll appreciate that could only be done incognito." The word Carol Hardman had used in the dark. Not a word he would normally have used himself, it had all the wrong connotations. But he had gone over that unique interview so many times.

"Tate *was* arrested, Inspector."

"And is being freed this morning. His alibi turned up. It was when I told your sister this, preparing her for the unpleasant processes it opened the way for, that she told me it was she who was guilty."

The face still hadn't changed, but he saw the lower lip tremble, and one of the hands on the desk, before it was slapped down on the leather surface with fingers spread.

"My sister was in Southampton that Saturday night." The voice was perhaps even quieter. "She came home for lunch on Sunday."

"Did you see her?"

"No," said Henry Payne reflectively. "She didn't come to the college. But surely other people—"

"Dr. Payne, I don't think you are quite realizing that it is Mrs. Hazell herself who has made the accusation. She would hardly tell me she was in London at lunchtime if someone had seen her at lunchtime in Bellfield."

His germ of an idea now was growing into recognizable shape.

"It's absurd. My sister must be mad. Temporarily mad. She has been deeply distressed over Juliet's death." *And you, sir?* "It has unhinged her. That is the only possible explanation." The voice was still calm. The hand that had trembled had picked up a ballpoint and was doodling on the margin of a typed sheet of paper.

"She didn't strike me as in any way mad," said Neil.

"She must be."

"You don't think she could possibly be telling the truth? She said it all happened without any—"

"Of course she couldn't be telling the truth. She worshipped the child."

It was a distinct shock to see the rolling tears, as unheralded as those shed by the sister. One of them fell on the back of the scribbling hand.

"You'll want to see her, of course. There will be no difficulty. You can simply—"

"Thank you for telling me these things, Inspector Carter." The tears in no way affected the quiet voice, or appeared to embarrass the speaker. "It can't have been easy. Now, if you'd leave me I should appreciate it."

"Of course, sir." Henry Payne's face seemed to have grown thinner in ten minutes. "Although I'm afraid I shall have to trouble you again later. I'm at Bellfield House now officially, and I shall have to take a further statement from you, as from Mr. Cowley and Miss Booth, when my detective sergeant arrives. So far as the students are concerned, of course, I'm still a civil servant on holiday. They'll all be gone in an hour." He hoped the dissembling journalist would be gone with them. "I'll tell them at breakfast that I've heard from you that your sister isn't feeling well this morning." He got to his feet. "So if you can be available during the morning, sir."

The reflexes of his changed position vis-à-vis Henry Payne and his staff were in working order.

"Of course, Inspector." Dr. Payne, too, seemed to have moved easily into the new relationship. "If you would like me to arrange for a room to be set aside for you here at the college?"

"That would be very helpful, sir. My wife and I will be going back to The Fallow Deer, but I should prefer to take statements at

Bellfield House. If you could manage not to say anything to Mr. Cowley and Miss Booth until I've spoken to them. I'll do that as soon as possible." He moved to the door, where he turned round. "I'm sorry, sir."

"Thank you, Inspector, of course."

The last thing he saw before he closed the door behind him was Henry Payne putting his face into his hands. Cathy had a space for him on one side of her at the breakfast table, Peter Cowley on the other. Miss Booth was absent, but he had hardly expected to find her still breakfasting at eight forty-five. One of the English Furniture people asked him if he had seen Mrs. Hazell.

"No, and I'm afraid we won't. The principal's just told me she's rung to say she isn't well this morning. Sends her good-byes and regrets at not having been able to mark your quiz papers," he added for good measure.

Under cover of the disappointed murmur—loudest, he fancied, from those who had thought they might have won—he gave Cathy a quick summary of his last few moments and their projected roles for the morning. He managed a piece of toast and a cup of coffee before Cowley got to his feet.

Neil stopped him in the dining-room doorway.

"Mr. Cowley, may I have a private word with you?"

"Yes, of course." There was no interest in this face either. "I've got plenty of time this morning. Plenty of time for weeks, my term's over. I'm going back to London this afternoon. Easter with my mother. Too much time."

"If we could go to your room." He almost called the youth "sir" too soon, and had to suppress a rogue impulse to laugh, on the instant of feeling he had never found a situation less funny. Cowley was probably thinking that "Peter" would be Neil's most natural form of address, in that hothouse atmosphere of shared cultural activity. All at once his desire to disabuse Cowley became uncomfortably urgent.

"It's a bit poky, but do sit here." In his narrow room, Cowley indicated the one small armchair as he passed round his desk and sat down. Behind him was another shrouded window, but to protect the lecturer from the view of those on the forecourt beyond, rather than veil the outdoors from the wandering attention of students.

He began, this time, with his deception, thinking Cowley would approve the reason for it and so be more inclined to cooperate. But the young man had evidently found it of comfort to concentrate his sorrow and fury onto Frank Tate, and withdrew his spontaneity. Coldly, then, Neil told him of Tate's release.

But not of Bertha Hazell's confession. As with Bertha, there was a dramatic separation of red and white in the attentive face.

"That means—" Cowley's fingertips were intertwined, the hands twisting backwards and forwards from the fixed point.

"It means, sir, that the case is now open again." Cowley would be thinking, of course, of his own presence that Sunday outside the flats where Juliet had died. Or even . . . But although it was so interesting to watch the quickening rise and fall of Cowley's chest, the panic in his eyes, he had to correct the lie implicit in what he had just said. "That is to say, it was open until Mrs. Hazell informed me last night that it was she who killed Juliet."

Amazement? Disbelief? Fear? Nothing in those large eyes, really, except the brilliant blue.

"Mrs. Hazell. But that's absurd . . ."

It wasn't in the eyes, perhaps it was in the way the hands had slackened and fallen quiet on the desk, that Neil was aware of relief.

"Mrs. Hazell has confessed to the murder of Juliet Payne, Mr. Cowley. I shall want to take a further statement from you in the specific area of Mrs. Hazell's movements. For instance, she said originally that she was back in Bellfield by lunchtime that Sunday, but if she went to London it would have to have been three o'clock at the earliest before—"

"I'm afraid I won't be able to help you there, Inspector." Cowley displayed a sudden boyish eagerness. "I was in London staying with my mother that Sunday. As you know."

Neil nodded. "As I know. I also know, Mr. Cowley, that you were outside the block of flats in Knightsbridge where Juliet Payne met her death, a few hours after that took place. I'm sorry you didn't see fit to mention this in your original statement."

"I . . ." The face now was all white.

"There's no doubt about it, Mr. Cowley."

There was doubt, of course, there was only Carol's word, but if Cowley didn't deny it, they could take her word.

"No." Cowley slumped back in his chair, his hands trailing off the desk into his lap. "I was there. I was trying to get up courage to call and see her. I'd asked her several times, at Bellfield, if I could see her when she came to London while I was staying with my mother, and although she hadn't said yes, she hadn't really said no, either. If you see what I mean."

"I think I do." Thinking of the letter, he saw quite easily.

"I thought I could just call, offer to take her to the station, be going casually by and deciding to drop in . . ."

The eyes pleaded, as if Neil could have supplied their owner with some of the sophistication possessed in such measure by his young ideal.

"And you decided against it?"

"I hadn't the courage. I decided I'd probably make things worse rather than better."

"Bad, were they?"

It was one of his infrequent rapier thrusts. Cowley retreated, gasping.

"No, no . . . They weren't— they weren't *anything.*"

"She was fifteen."

"I know, I know. I never forgot that, it was just that . . . I worshipped her, Mr. Carter."

And touched the hem of her garment? Did something, at least, to give her power? The letter had gone back to London with Bob Ryan. Anyway, he must be concerned with Cowley now only in so far as he could throw light on Bertha Hazell.

"Thank you for telling me, Mr. Cowley." One of his, Neil's, strengths. People did tell him things. About themselves, if not about the cases in which they were concerned. There was a knock at the door. Miss Booth's head came round.

"Ah, Mr. Carter! There's someone here to see you. A Mr. Hughes."

Neil started to speak, then stopped and looked at Cowley. Cowley got to his feet and asked Miss Booth to show Mr. Hughes in.

"Perhaps you would be good enough to come in too, Miss

Booth," suggested Neil. Her teeth were hidden, but the predation was in her eyes. It was good to see David entering the room behind her, tall and fair and readable. "This is Detective Sergeant Hughes, and I'm Detective Inspector Carter. Both of the Metropolitan Police."

Miss Booth's eyes were green ice. "I'm afraid I don't understand."

He went through it again. His deception and the reason for it. Frank Tate's release, justifying his unease. Bertha Hazell's confession.

Miss Booth was excited by his revelations. Her lips parted quite early on, showing those small white spears. He knew how unfair he was being, seeing them as a factor in the investigation. Feeling sorry despite himself for Peter Cowley with his soft fair hair and bruised, bewildered look. Falling victim to the cuddly-bunny syndrome, for goodness' sake.

Neither of them was of much help. When he and David had him on his own, Cowley amended his original statement about his whereabouts in London on the afternoon of the Sunday in question, and reiterated that Miss Booth had informed him by telephone at his mother's, during the evening, of what had happened in the Knightsbridge flat. He hadn't seen Mrs. Hazell until his return to college on the Tuesday evening, when they had—well, they had just put their arms round one another and shed tears. As if in illustration, Peter Cowley shed them again. Yes, Mrs. Hazell had been very distressed, even distraught, but he had thought that in the circumstances this was to be expected.

Miss Booth hadn't seen Bertha Hazell that Sunday either.

"No, of course not. You didn't come to the college at all that day, did you, Miss Booth?" Miss Booth lived in Lyndhurst, although she had a room to sleep in at the college if working especially late or especially early. Not having been present when she made her first statement, Neil was glad of the chance to recap where he could.

Although why should he want to do that?

"No, not that Sunday, although some Sundays I did." Miss Booth's excitement had died down, she looked neat and composed.

"You didn't come to Bellfield at all, in fact. You were"—he looked down at the pages in front of him, although it was already in his mind what he was going to say—"at home. Your sister came to see you."

"Yes, Inspector." Her lips were together, and he had his second brief wish to unpin her hair. He wished, too, that he could ask her if she and her sister had seen or spoken to anyone . . .

Henry Payne told them that on second thoughts he had an idea he had seen his sister round about lunchtime, but when Neil reminded him that he had lunched with a visiting friend who could be asked to search his memory too, he reported reluctantly that he realized he had not been in touch with her that day until the police arrived with their terrible news and he telephoned her. He was convinced her shock and her grief had been genuine.

That had been at about five o'clock. Bertha Hazell had said so too, in both her statements.

"As I told you earlier, Inspector, a temporary insanity."

"You wish to see her of course, sir?"

"Of course, yes." But Henry Payne looked slightly surprised. Neil wondered if his mind was now consolingly gripped by some controversial aspect of classical architecture.

"You'll go this afternoon?"

"Yes, I can go this afternoon. I have no teaching today."

After telling David to set Dr. Payne on his way and complete the paperwork to do with the statements, Neil walked the short way to The Fallow Deer without going back upstairs—Cathy had taken the suitcases and the car and reinstalled them in the hotel.

The morning weather had passed without him seeing it, and as the sun warmed his face and he smelt the hedgerows, he felt again the vague sense of regret which had visited him early on the stairs. It was a glorious day.

Cathy was in the garden behind the hotel, sketching. It seemed ages since he had seen her.

"Neil! What is it, darling?"

Suddenly overwhelmed by the thought of her waiting for him, of her being there waiting, if he was good to her, so long as they both lived, he was trembling.

"Only that I'm glad to see you."

"I thought perhaps your head . . ."

"My head's all right, I'd forgotten about it. I'm glad I forgot about the plaster when I was being official."

And even though the case was apparently wrapped up again he must still be official, revealing his true role to the management and making sure he would be found if there was a telephone call, looking in on the local station to explain developments, arranging for David to join him and Cathy for lunch, deciding afterwards he ought to think aloud to David rather than to his wife before sending him with the statements back to London.

The three of them went to the Carters' room first to hear on the news that Frank Tate had been released and that a further arrest seemed imminent. Nothing more, to Neil's apparently illogical relief. In the garden, in the sunshine which was almost hot, Cathy sat down with her sketchbook just out of earshot of the teak garden seat where the two policemen installed themselves.

"Presumably you've got views by now, governor, on Bertha Hazell? Was this a surprise?"

"Absolutely. In fact, David . . ."

David was dubious about his idea, but the exercise of putting it into words convinced Neil it was worth trying. If his chief wasn't able to tell him one or two things . . .

"Well, Neil, only you can decide. That was an extraordinary thing with Carol Hardman."

"Luck, really." But it was pleasant to see the admiration in David's eyes, telling him his junior was putting the scoop down to him, rather than to chance. "Perhaps a bit more than luck as regards the letter. I found it wedged inside a cupboard in the Wendy house at the bottom of the garden. Bob Ryan admitted they hadn't looked round the garden. It went back with him in the night, but here's a copy I scribbled while we were waiting." While Cathy and Bertha were making the second lot of tea.

David whistled. "Juliet?"

"Not a doubt of it. I was sure right away, but there was an exercise book in her desk which confirmed it."

"Cowley?"

"I can't think who else. But of course it may never have been sent. For heaven's sake, take your jacket off." The glisten on David's top lip was beginning to bead. "I'd confront him with it, if the case wasn't closed again—there must have been something which made her go as far as a draft."

"You're still not happy?"

The question, this time, wasn't being posed while he was half asleep, but he couldn't really vary his answer. "Ah, David, I don't feel happy about anything to do with Juliet Payne."

"But surely if Mrs. Hazell actually confessed . . ."

"Yes, yes. But if the chief can't reassure me on certain things . . . My God, it's her stepson."

Neil had thought at first, if he had thought anything, that the tall neat figure in the dark suit, strolling across the lawn, was an under manager.

"Mr. Hazell." He was on his feet and walking forward to meet John Hazell. "What brings you here on a working day?"

"Detective Inspector Carter." So Hazell had been to the college, or in touch with the chief. The voice was perhaps not quite so lazy and there was some colour in the face, the unattractive light pink which is usually the only colour vouchsafed to the putty-toned.

Neil waited. There was no point in prompting Hazell with information he didn't have.

"I tried to telephone Bertha early this morning, and when there was no reply I rang the college. They told me she'd stayed at home because she wasn't well. When her telephone was checked there was nothing wrong with it. So I came down. If I'd spoken to Miss Booth in the first place, I'd have saved myself the journey. She told me what has happened."

Neil thought he could sense anger, tightly controlled. Anger at his stepmother for behaviour either criminal or lunatic? At Neil for his deception? "That's right, sir." He realized how desirably defusing the title could be. "When I told her Tate's alibi had turned up and he was to be released, she immediately confessed to the murder." Hazell was turning a cold eye on David at Neil's side. "This is Detective Sergeant Hughes, my colleague."

There was no acknowledgement. Hazell had returned his gaze to Neil. "And you, Inspector, were behaving somewhat unethically. You lied your way into my stepmother's house."

Their eyes met on the exact level.

"Yes. Because I wasn't satisfied about Tate's arrest and I wanted to see Juliet's background for myself, without alerting her family. I was on holiday, Mr. Hazell, until I was put in charge of the Bellfield end of the investigation. Events have justified my uneasiness."

"And now you can relax. Bertha must be mad." For a flash, the anger reached the eyes.

It wasn't quite what Henry Payne had said.

"You think she could have done this thing, sir?"

"I imagine there to be several hundred people who could have done it, Inspector, but Bertha has apparently been the one to own up."

"Yes, sir." Turning his head slightly, he saw that Cathy was busy over her sketch pad. "If there is any help you are able to give us with regard to your stepmother's movements on the Sunday in question, we would appreciate it if you would be prepared to make a statement."

"Of course, Inspector, but I hardly think there is anything helpful I can say. Bertha and I were very intermittently in touch. We were more likely to meet, if we met, when she came to London than by my coming here. But if she was in London that Sunday, she didn't get in touch with me."

"I see, sir. Thank you. It would be helpful, perhaps, if you could tell me your reason for telephoning her this morning." Hazell was one of those people who made him hate the necessity at times of sounding deferential. "Anything you could tell me would be—"

"Inspector Carter." Patience was being less and less easily imposed on that profound anger. "I'm sure I don't have to tell you anything about my stepmother's current condition. Even without her extraordinary confession it was obvious to me at the weekend that she was in an unstable state." Had John Hazell never seen Bertha present her treasures to a group of students? "I told her I would keep in touch—you may have heard me, you were there when I left. To tell you the truth, I was a bit concerned about her."

So the cold bastard only waited three days before telephoning.

Again, as John Hazell shifted slightly, it was a surprise to smell his cologne.

"Of course, sir. Unless you feel you can give us any help regarding the elusive personality of Juliet Payne"—was this a fair entreaty?—"there's no need to detain you. If you rarely come to Bellfield, I suppose you hardly ever—"

"I can't remember when I last saw Juliet, Inspector." The face had regained its customary pallor. "Bertha suggested a month or so ago that I might take the child out to lunch on one of her London Sundays, and perhaps I would have got round to it. However . . ."

John Hazell spread his hands and ruefully smiled. His smile was no more disarming than Miss Booth's, even though his mouth and teeth were attractive. Perhaps it was the contrast with the cool, dark eyes.

"Of course, sir. It doesn't seem as if there is anything you can tell us."

"She was a nice little girl." The words came with uncharacteristic spontaneity, as if they had to be said. "When my father was alive, I was here more often, especially in the early days of his marriage to Bertha. I tried to teach her—Juliet—to play croquet, but the mallets were too heavy." John Hazell blinked; perhaps there was a spark of feeling which he wanted to veil, perhaps he had sometimes made up the party lunching at The Master Builder in Buckler's Hard, had gone to tell Juliet her meal was getting cold when she had danced out of the hotel to monitor the ponies . . . "It was rather inconvenient for me to come down today, Inspector, so if you will excuse me . . ."

"Of course, Mr. Hazell. Dr. Payne, by the way, has gone to London to see his sister."

"So Miss Booth told me. You're staying down here, Inspector?"

"For the time being."

He would be, if the chief didn't play. He felt a pang as he realized he was more anxious to be allowed to go to London than to continue his honeymoon. Before David left with the statements, Cathy showed them the sketches she had made. She had caught Neil's impatience. When they had seen David off, he took her back into the garden and told her what he wanted to do.

"I'll be back by late afternoon, darling." But he shouldn't be more willing to give up time with her because there was going to be so much of it.

"Of course. I hope your chief says yes. It's an awfully good idea."

The chief, when telephoned, it was immediately clear, was in a particularly prickly mood. Neil began by telling him about John Hazell's visit. He thought it diffused the ill humour a little.

"So how is it with Mrs. Hazell, governor?"

The growl was not encouraging, but he persisted.

"You've matched fingerprints?"

"No."

"She's told you something the public couldn't know. About the clock—"

"She hasn't."

"Somebody round about the flats recognized her mug shot."

"They didn't."

"She must have filled up with petrol, governor. Surely a service station—"

"She filled up on Saturday night, on her way to Southampton."

A gloomy relish was mounting in the chief's voice.

"So what do you think, governor?"

"I don't know, Neil. We haven't charged her yet."

It was all the encouragement he needed. "Before you do, Governor . . ." He said it swiftly and fluently, he knew exactly what he was going to say.

The chief was silent a few moments, but when he spoke his tone was comparatively mild. "I'm not sure of the ethics, Neil."

Ethics was a word the chief had probably learned from him, Neil. He wouldn't be deterred by having it used against him, John Hazell had already done that. He'd been unethical, anyway, all the way through this wretched case. "You're not sure of Mrs. Hazell's ethics, either, governor. The thing is, it'll work."

He prayed into the second pause, and eventually the chief said, grudgingly, "All right, then."

"Thank you, governor. I know it'll be difficult over the flat—"

"It won't be difficult over the flat. The Hardmans have gone to the seaside. Taken Carol. The flat's empty. Make it by eleven."

The chief could so easily have said ten, or even nine. It could be he thought Neil had a good idea.

"May I have the evening off, governor?"

"I suppose so. Eleven sharp. Remember me to your wife."

They told The Fallow Deer they were sorry not to have announced earlier that they would be out for dinner, and went to Brockenhurst for the gourmet delights of Carey's Manor. Then walked about the forest clearings hand in hand until it was dark. It seemed a long time since he had had something definite to do which was likely to solve a problem and which could not be influenced one way or another by anything he might think about it. He had one of the best evenings of his life.

CHAPTER 13

He made it to the office by ten to eleven. Not, when it came to it, in the least wanting to go. Not wanting to leave Cathy and the forest, which in the sun-shot gloom of the early-morning bedroom had seemed one benevolent entity.

Bertha Hazell was awaiting him in an interview room, getting slowly to her feet as he went in. She was more untidy than the usual slight disorder of her daytime self, her white cotton blouse offering the probably reliable indication that she had slept in it. The gold chain still shaped her throat. There seemed to be more grey in her scarcely brushed brown hair, but that was probably the effect of the electric light in the windowless room, rather than the toll of events. He was aware, too, of an inner disarray. It was hard to believe he had so recently and so humbly sat at her feet.

"Good morning, Mrs. Hazell." Again, he was grateful that his revealed professional role presented them with a defined relationship.

"Inspector Carter. You wanted to see me." He had been braced for scorn in her eyes, if not on her tongue, but it was as if she had no reaction to him.

"I did, yes. I want to ask you if you will come with me and my sergeant to the flat in Knightsbridge where your niece's death took place. There are one or two details which are not quite clear to us, and it would be helpful."

There was no mistaking the horror, and then the fear, which flashed across her eyes.

"Must I?"

He repeated firmly, "It would be helpful," and fixed her gaze until it dropped. She said quietly, to her twisting hands, "All right."

"Thank you." He moved to the door and opened it. "Tell Ser-

geant Hughes, will you, constable." The WPC who had been sitting unobtrusively across the room got to her feet and joined him
in the doorway. "If you're ready, Mrs. Hazell. Don't forget your
cardigan." It was the heavy-knit brown one she had tended to
leave behind on the backs of chairs at Bellfield House. He saw
gooseflesh on her arms. "Better put it on."

When they were all out of the room, the WPC sped off. David
joined them at the end of a short silence in which Neil had found
himself thinking it was unfair that he shouldn't have to ask her
pardon. For lying his way into her house. Her stepson had put it
succinctly.

David gave him one old-fashioned look, supporting the idea
Neil had had in the garden of The Fallow Deer that David's
moral sense was uneasy at what Neil had persuaded the chief to
let him do. David and Mrs. Hazell sat in the back of the car, and
nobody talked except about the best way to get to the flats.

"Where was it you parked?" asked Neil as the curly red façade
came in sight.

"Sorry?" She leaned forward. He wondered if she was gaining
time.

"I asked you where you parked, Mrs. Hazell."

"Oh, down the side." They were level with a side road where
two delivery vans were spaced on the single yellow line. "This
side. As I said, no single yellow line restrictions on a Sunday."

"On Fridays there are." He wasn't driving a police car. He
would park on the private ground at the back of the block. He
said, as he turned between the ornate red posts, "You didn't think
of coming in here, Mrs. Hazell?"

"I didn't know it existed. I'd never been here before, it was just
an address."

"Of course, yes." Had she, so far, been lucky? If so, her luck
couldn't hold.

The porter in the bottle-green uniform had the flat key in his
hand by the time Neil had his ID out. He would probably have
been able to tell them how Carol Hardman was, but Neil didn't
ask. He asked Mrs. Hazell, in the lift, to refresh his memory: had
she gone up in it that other time?

"Yes, Mr. Carter, I went up in the lift. It's in my statement."

"Your revised statement, yes. We'll just go through it all as it happened, Mrs. Hazell." He didn't want to alert her at the crucial point, better she should feel she had to be on her guard the whole time. "I'm sorry to subject you to what I know must be something of an ordeal, but I do assure you it's important."

"If you say so." She and David, at the same moment, raised their heads to the ornate gilded ceiling of the slowly clanking lift. He had always gauged his sanity on the way he could note small things which, in other contexts, would have been funny. "But I can't really see . . . I've told you what happened, Inspector Carter, I'm not trying to pretend I'm innocent."

Ah no, he didn't think she was trying to pretend that. "Of course not, Mrs. Hazell, and I regret the necessity for this exercise. It's just that one or two things are still not quite clear." He tried to smile reassuringly. At least Cathy wasn't having to share his discomfort. "You didn't see anyone on the landing?"

"I told you, I didn't see anyone anywhere." She was paler than he had yet seen her, and breathing like an asthmatic. He hoped she wouldn't collapse on them.

"Don't worry." He took her arm, then released it in case she failed to recognize the gesture as unofficial.

The name *Hardman* had been restored on the front door of flat number twenty-nine. He was in the hall before he realized that he, too, could be in danger of collapse. It hadn't occurred to him that he would be setting up an ordeal for two, that he would have to fight his own wave of giddiness and nausea.

He must have shown something, because David's arm, unobtrusively, was across his back.

"Shall I take Mrs. Hazell into the bedroom, governor, while you—"

"Thank you, Sergeant, we'll all go into the bedroom." The inrush of anger at his weakness had done the trick, dispersing it as swiftly as it had come. "Mrs. Hazell." He was walking towards the bedroom and she had stopped and was looking about her as if she was in a dream. David took her arm and led her across the hall.

Neil indicated the small armchair by the window and she took it. She still looked dazed. "Now, Mrs. Hazell, if you'll just go through things as they happened. Just as you told me, as you put it in your amended statement. It won't take long. Your niece ran in here, and you followed her . . ."

"That's right." She looked up at him, standing with David in front of her, with something of her old spirit. She went through it as she had gone through it at her cottage, he thought in many of the same phrases. When she had finished, she looked down at her hands, putting them together as if, united, they might stop trembling.

"Thank you," said Neil gently. David had moved close to an open pane of window. "Yes, I think we've got the picture clearly now. Juliet ran in here and you—attacked her—on this bed."

She nodded, not looking up.

"If you could just answer me, Mrs. Hazell."

Her chin shot high. "I have answered you, and your colleagues, I've answered you over and over again. I followed Juliet in here. I attacked her—I killed her—on that bed. Will you never be satisfied?"

"I am satisfied, Mrs. Hazell." He crouched down on the floor in front of her, separated her hands into his. Now he had won, he could concentrate on being merciful. "I'm satisfied that you didn't kill your niece. You see, she wasn't killed in this room, she was killed next door, in the master bedroom."

He didn't know what he had expected, but never the burst of laughter. Pulling her hands away, Mrs. Hazell sat helplessly laughing.

"I'm sorry." He got to his feet and stood uneasily watching her.

"Oh, don't be sorry, Mr. Carter." Mrs. Hazell found a handkerchief, wiped her eyes and blew her nose. "Another dirty trick. I should have known."

"Forgive me." Her description of his ploy was a shock, implying a reaction she hadn't shown him. "There was no evidence against you beyond your self-accusation, and I found I just couldn't believe it. Why did you accuse yourself?" He went to sit on the end of the bed, without hesitation in this room of no associations.

"No law says I must explain." She spoke calmly.

"That is so. But I can't believe you are any less anxious than I am to get at the truth of Juliet's death." Her eyes faltered, were suddenly luminous with tears. "I think you did what you did, Mrs. Hazell, for the best reason. I think you wanted to protect someone you care for."

He fell silent, watching her. Now at last her hands were still, every part of her was motionless, waiting for what else he had to say. The tears had dried as quickly as they had flooded, and there was no expression in her eyes.

"If you saw Peter Cowley that Sunday," said David from the window, "you must amend your statement. If he was near these flats it doesn't mean he killed your niece. Any more than it means you did, if you were near them."

Mrs. Hazell's second paroxysm of laughter was no less of a shock. She said this time, as she recovered, "You policemen are too clever, really you are. But I didn't see Peter. I couldn't have seen him, I wasn't here. I didn't come to London, I thought about it, but I didn't come; when I left Peggy's I went home. I didn't see anyone, except for a couple of people I didn't know passing the cottage when I was in the garden. I hoped no one had seen me."

"It appears that no one had, Mrs. Hazell." David had come away from the window.

"Mr. Carter." She seemed more composed than she had been all morning. "You must believe me when I tell you that I don't know anything about Peter. I was just afraid . . . I knew how fond he was of Juliet, and knowing now what I know about her . . . I just thought he might have found out. Or—or—that she might have behaved . . ." Mrs. Hazell shook her head and looked down at her hands, once more twisting together. "I felt I could cope better. I didn't mind what happened to me any more except for getting on with the book I'm writing about chairs and I could have done that in prison—or hospital"—briefly she faltered —"and when you said it was possible that I could have done it, I said I had. I know it was foolish, but I thought that whatever Peter might have done would have been because Juliet . . . not because he . . ."

His first thought had been of mother love, but what if she had thought of Cowley in another way? Carol Hardman had said Miss

Booth had a shine to him. Both women could have been jealous . . .

"That's all right, Mrs. Hazell. You haven't done any harm to Peter Cowley, I assure you. You've merely hampered and delayed our investigations. However, I don't anticipate any charges being brought. I'm not going back to Bellfield until this evening, but I'll be very glad to give you a lift home then if you want to stay in London for the day—"

"Thank you, Inspector Carter." Bertha Hazell got to her feet. "I would prefer to go straight home. If you will take me back to your headquarters so that I can collect my things and be signed off or whatever happens, I'll get a train."

"Yes, of course." He was suddenly afraid she might ask to see the murder bed. Escorting her to freedom, he felt he could take her arm, and he steered her steadily across the hall and out of the flat. He thought he was sparing her as well as himself when he asked David to run her to Waterloo.

The chief was eating a batch at his desk. Neil declined his suggestion that another should be sent for, but accepted coffee. The chief said they should bring Cowley in for questioning, before Neil got round to mentioning it.

"He's back in London with his mother, governor. If I was to call on him. Background."

"What about your wife, Neil?"

Neil, too, had remembered Cathy. "My wife will understand, governor. I'll telephone her before I go off for Cowley."

He told her exactly how it was. When she said, with a laugh, "Perhaps it's just as well Bertha Hazell was the only person we told we were on our honeymoon," she wasn't being sarcastic. She went on to say that of course he must be the person to question Peter Cowley.

"If I'm not home for dinner I'll be home for bed. I love you more this moment than at any other time."

"I know. I'm going to take my paints into the garden."

Time was saved by Cowley being at home in his mother's Edwardian mansion flat in Bayswater. And Neil's feelings by the mother being out, although really he would have liked to meet her. There was no mistaking the fear which had leapt in Cowley's large blue eyes. And then again when he saw David.

"Inspector Carter. I did tell you I was coming back to London—"

"You did, sir, which was very helpful."

David came level with Neil. He was just able to do this in the narrow hall, made narrower by the looming bulk of an ornate black sideboard of Victorian Tudor. Neil's imagining of what Mrs. Hazell would have made of it was tinged with regret.

"We should be glad, sir," said David, "if you would agree to come with us to the Yard to answer a few further questions."

Cowley cast a swift glance behind him, as if in instinctive measurement of the distance to any unattended door.

"Mrs. Hazell . . ."

"Mrs. Hazell has retracted her statement, Mr. Cowley," continued David.

"If she saw me, it could only have been—"

"Mrs. Hazell didn't see you, sir. Now, if you would be good enough to come along with us we'd appreciate it."

"It really is best," said Neil.

"I shan't be retracting *my* statement, Inspector." It was the only faintly mutinous stance Cowley had taken, and it immediately collapsed.

"All the same, sir," said Neil, "I should bring a coat." It was one of the things he liked least about his job, the way suspects in their nervousness lost their basic abilities to look after themselves.

"Of course, yes." Cowley pulled a raincoat from a curving prong of the hallstand which matched the sideboard.

The chief decided, when Neil did him the courtesy of informing him that Cowley was *in situ,* to present the letter to him in person. Normally Neil enjoyed watching the chief at his amiable deadly game of interrogation, but this case, even in this respect, was different. At least he had managed to avoid being around while Cowley was submitted to fingerprinting. He could see black traces still outlining Cowley's unique whorls, where his hands fidgeted on the table top.

"Have a look at this, Cowley," beamed the chief, slipping the sheet of paper under the stained fingertips.

If it had been a film, Neil would have called Cowley a ham actor. Except that he could hardly have summoned up the changes of colour in his face as he cried, "No! I can't believe . . ." and dropped his head on his hands.

"All right now," said the chief. "We'll order some tea and you can tell us about it."

So the letter had been sent. When Cowley had taken several sips of tea, the chief asked him straight out.

"Yes. I found it on my desk. Sealed in an envelope, of course."

"Where is it now, Mr. Cowley?"

"I . . . Oh, what's the use?" The mutiny flared even more briefly than in the hall of his mother's house. "I burned it. I'd got it with me in London, and when Miss Booth rang me and told me what had happened to Juliet, I burned it."

"Why did you do that, Mr. Cowley?" The chief was still apparently relaxed, still smiling his deadly smile.

"Because I didn't want anyone to know Juliet had written it, that she'd . . ."

"Why did she write it?"

Cowley really did bear out the cliché of the trapped animal.

"I don't know why she wrote it. There was nothing, I swear there was nothing. I don't pretend I wasn't . . . I didn't . . . I worshipped her. I thought we were starting to be friends. We used to go for walks sometimes—you'll know that." No, they hadn't known it, it hadn't been in that first statement which at the time had been merely put on file. "Then one day—just once, two or three weeks ago—she started running and asked me to catch her and she suddenly ran up to a tree and turned with her back against it and her face up—oh God—and I had to stop suddenly and my face was near her and I—I kissed her. Oh, nothing, it was nothing, but she seemed to be asking. I swear . . ."

Cowley's head went down again, and the chief waited. In the silence the frustrated buzzing of a bluebottle on the window sounded very loud.

"What was Juliet Payne's reaction at the time, Mr. Cowley?" The chief spoke softly, as Cowley's head slowly rose.

"She— didn't say anything. She just turned her head away and walked away from the tree. I didn't say anything either. She seemed quite calm, I remember I thought she even seemed—well, pleased if anything—and although I knew I shouldn't have done it and I told myself I wouldn't do it again, whatever"—*whatever the provocation*—"I remember I felt happy. *Happy.*" Cowley almost groaned.

"So the letter was a shock to you, Mr. Cowley?"

"A shock? It was a terrible shock, I couldn't . . . I hadn't recovered from the shock when Miss Booth telephoned and told me . . ." If it had been a film with anything like artistic pretensions, Cowley's head would not have been allowed to go down for the third time.

"Yet you went to the block of flats in Knightsbridge where she was staying, Mr. Cowley." The chief's voice was hardening. "You said in your amended statement that you hung about there hoping to see her."

"That was *why* . . . I hadn't seen her since I'd had the letter, at least I'd only see her going through doors, sliding round corners, just out of reach, out of earshot . . ." Neil could imagine it, he could see the blond, bewildered teddy bear reaching out to the small, perpetually disappearing figure. "I told you I couldn't get my courage up to call on her in the flat, but I thought that if I could see her coming out—well, I was bound to see her, and if I caught her unawares, she might give me some idea of why she'd written that letter, what she really felt . . ."

What Juliet really felt. Neil realized, on a sense of depressed resignation, that this was something none of them would ever know.

"Yes, Mr. Cowley, I believe you that the letter you had received from Juliet Payne was the reason why you went to the flats in Knightsbridge. But I think you went there much earlier than you were seen outside and I think you went into the building and up to the flat and rang the bell and were let in—"

"I didn't! I wasn't! I didn't go near the place until the afternoon. Anyway, if I had got my courage up, I thought the people who lived in the flat would be there too. I didn't know Juliet was alone, I didn't know what she and the other girl . . . did . . ."

"Didn't you, Mr. Cowley? I suggest that Juliet Payne had done more than send you a letter, I suggest she had subsequently told you the real story, and that you knew she would be alone—"

"No, no! I didn't know!"

"All right, Mr. Cowley, I put another possibility to you." The chief's smile, now, was one Neil was grateful not to be receiving. "I suggest you are telling the truth when you say you didn't know, when you say you thought the people who lived in the flat would be there. I suggest you did in fact pluck up courage, as you said in your amended statement you had failed to do"—somehow Neil couldn't imagine the chief studying the statements, the case seemed to be privately his, Neil's, case—"and went up to the flat before lunchtime, perhaps in the hope of being invited for a drink, or even for lunch, and then having Juliet to yourself by escorting her to the station. When she answered the door in the character of —er—Marilyn, and you realized she was alone, your shock and your outrage were such that, unwitnessed, you—"

"No, no! I didn't, I swear I didn't!"

"Or possibly," continued the chief implacably, "you telephoned the flat in advance and Juliet asked you to come. That would account for her telling Detective Inspector Carter, when she telephoned him, that she was expecting someone." It would indeed account for it. No suggested solution of the mystery had yet been so plausible. So why didn't it make him feel any happier? It must be more than Cowley's air of vulnerability, or he was going soft. How would he feel if Miss Booth was sitting at bay in Cowley's place? "Then you came back in the afternoon to see if anyone had—"

"No. Oh no. I didn't. I've told you the truth. I *did* get that letter. I *didn't* see Juliet properly between getting it and going to London. I *didn't*—know about her. I *didn't* go to those flats before lunch. And when I went in the afternoon, I didn't go into the building." Cowley put a hand up to each side of his head and shook it as if it was separate from him. The action was evidently helpful. Suddenly he was glaring at the chief. "Why don't you talk to Mary Booth? I used to see her sometimes when I was walking with Juliet. Walking on her own. She never came up to us, she just stood half behind trees or sort of went on walking parallel to us. Sometimes she'd appear when Juliet and I were talking in the

house or the garden. She made me uncomfortable when I was
alone with her, she was too nice to me. She didn't like Juliet. She
knew what I thought about Juliet and she couldn't be rude to her
because of who Juilet was . . . Oh Lord." Cowley shook his
head again, without benefit of his hands, and looked appalled.
Neil thought he had just talked against his normal good nature. A
measure of his desperation to be believed. Because he was telling
the truth? Or because he was afraid of it?

"All right, Mr. Cowley, we're not concerned with Miss Booth
at the moment, we're concerned—very much concerned—with
you. It will save a lot of time and trouble if you tell us about your
first visit to the flat in Knightsbridge . . ."

It went on like that for another hour, and then the chief left and
it went on like that for another hour with Neil and David. At
some point word came that Cowley's fingerprints didn't match
with anything in the flat, but of course, although this meant he
wasn't convicted, it didn't mean he was exonerated. Doors, chair
arms, glasses, could have been wiped, or might not have been
touched. And if there'd been premeditation—from the start,
which Neil couldn't really believe, or at some stage of an encounter—then there were such things as gloves . . .

When Cowley, unyielding, had signed his third and, he swore,
his totally true, statement, he was allowed to go. No sign of grace,
though; no one ran him home.

"I hope you've no plans to go far from London, Mr. Cowley,"
said Neil.

"Only to Bellfield. I hope that's in order." Cowley's attempt to
be dignified was upsetting. If nothing and nobody else came up,
the poor bastard would be a suspect for the rest of his life.

"Of course you may go to Bellfield. You're thinking of going
now?"

"Not now." Cowley pushed the floppy hair off his damp forehead. "I was thinking of next term." He had seen the long prospect. Neil couldn't even reassure him that the secret of the letter
was safe with the police; they'd have to ask Dr. Payne and Bertha
Hazell if they knew anything about it, and anything about Cowley
vis-à-vis Juliet between the time he'd said he received it and his
departure on holiday to London . . .

The chief told Neil with apparent good humour that he could go back to the country.

"Take the weekend off, Neil, look after your wife. We'll have to get going down in the forest again on Monday, think I'll go down myself. Perhaps you'll have had enough of it." The chief could be surprisingly perceptive. Unless it was that he himself was getting interested.

"Yes, governor, I think we'll come back to town tomorrow."

And today . . . It was only just after half past three.

When he got downstairs he didn't go for his car, he went out into the street on foot and took the tube to Tottenham Court Road.

CHAPTER 14

The flat was on the top floor of a terraced house the rest of which was occupied by a university department. A young woman at a desk in the narrow hallway told him to go up as far as he could. The first three flights were rubber-tipped, and men and women glanced out at him, smiling or blank, as he passed their open doors. There was a smell of duplicating ink and stationery which halfway up the fourth flight of shabbily carpeted stairs was superseded by another, more obtrusive, smell which he disliked but, as on his first visit, couldn't quite define. Fabrics and furniture too long undisturbed? Old age? Had Juliet's nose wrinkled as she climbed each month to her music master's eyrie?

The old woman answered his ring. He had to tell her a couple of times it was all right, before her anxious face cleared. The smell was worse once he was inside the narrow passageway, worse, he thought, than last time. The pattern of the carpet was almost lost under dust; dust waved in fungus-shaped arcs on the darkly papered walls. Juliet must have seen that; had she felt sorry?

He followed the old woman into the sitting room. It felt strange to be reminded through the small window that he was still in central London. The furniture was dull-surfaced and heavy, there were a lot of haphazardly hung and predominantly sepia photographs—now he no longer wanted the usual things from them, he could more clearly see their surroundings. The grand piano stood in the centre of the room, alone among the contents in emitting a faint mahogany shine.

The old man, very still in an armchair, knew him after no more than a few seconds' hesitation. Neil despised the squeamishness which made him want to refuse the old woman's offer of tea while accepting it.

"This visit," he said, drawing an upright chair close to the old man as she shuffled out to the hall, "isn't because of any official interest in you. I'm privately interested because I hope that perhaps you can help me."

"I . . . help you?" The thin face hadn't coarsened with age. It was easy to imagine how this man had looked, as long as fifty years ago. The ginger-grey hair was neatly combed, but that could be accomplished by feel. The trouble in the flat now must be old eyes. He'd get in touch with the local department, see if someone tactful could suggest a home help . . . "Ah. You mean you hope to discover what the child was like. I have thought about that, Mr. Carter, for most of the time since she died. And before she died. And still I do not know."

He had hardly expected anything else, but the disappointment was physical.

"You had no idea—" Of course the old man had had no idea, of course he hastened to tell Neil so. "Tell me at least, you can tell me this. Did she change?"

"Ah!" When the old man moved, a little puff of dust rose between his thigh and the vaguely patterned cushion beneath him. "She did change, yes. Anna and I talked of it."

The old woman was coming back already into the room carrying a tray set with tea for one in a pretty flowered tea set, on a stained but beautifully embroidered white cloth. He imagined some perpetually brooding urn, of vaguely East European design.

"Of what, *Liebchen?*" The tea, fussed over by both husband and wife, was set down on a small table at his side. The old man had grown narrower since he had bought his trousers. Or perhaps they had been bought by someone else.

"Of the child Juliet. Of the change in her."

"*Ach,* yes." The hazed eyes stared sadly towards him. Not even in Bertha Hazell's bedroom could the thought of Juliet hang more palpably. Wanting to disturb it, he poured and sipped some tea.

"So she changed?" The tea had been all right in his mouth, but was burning his chest. "When?"

"Two or three years ago, I should say, Mr. Carter. Oh, she was always a little grave, a little serious. But she could smile properly at first. Even laugh as a child laughs."

"Was it suddenly one Saturday?" It sounded like the title of a melodrama.

"Yes, that is what it was. One Saturday she came, and she was different. I remember you asked her, *Liebchen*"—the face which had first called forth affectionate diminutives was lost now inside a benevolent circle of flesh—"you asked her what was wrong."

He felt the excitement in his fingertips. "You remember that. You remember her answer?"

"I remember there was no answer." The old man's wistful eyes were fixed a long way off. He thought a second time of Bertha Hazell. "She said she was all right, she raised her shoulders and she stared at Anna. Then at me. She told us in that way, Inspector, not to ask her again. We never did. And she was never again as she had been at first. She smiled—perhaps she smiled more widely, I do not see faces quite clearly—but just with her lips. You understand?"

He understood, for certain now, that something had happened.

"I think so. Thank you. Did her music change?"

"Never." As at the other time he had been here, the old man's eyes swam at the mention of Juliet's music. "That is to say, it improved. All the time, it improved. She was a clever girl, Miss Juliet. She knew that she improved, but she didn't care. You understand? It puzzled me that she could be so good, get better, and still not care. If she had cared . . . Ah, she would have then been a great pianist. I am sure of it."

And at her death this old heart, for one, would have broken. Neil realized he had learned, through his own reactions, something of the nature of obsession.

He hadn't quite finished the cup of tea he had poured out, but he got to his feet. "Thank you. Thank you both very much. No one will trouble you again. I know you've suffered."

"For the child. We have suffered for the child." Sighing, the old man got to his feet, putting his hand out pettishly to the old woman in a gesture of dismissal as she began to move towards the door, and, smiling at Neil, she stood back. In the passageway Neil shook the thin yellow hand, wondering if it still played as well as illustrating lessons. Wondering vaguely, his thoughts were already moving towards the second of his self-imposed visits.

It was only five o'clock; if he went back for his car now, he would be with Cathy for dinner. The seventh dinner of their married lives. But on the pavement outside the house, with the wraith of a face at the top window, he hesitated only a few seconds. Then he went back to Tottenham Court Road and took the Northern Line south under the river.

Tate probably wouldn't be at home. And if he was, he'd have even less to say than the old man. He had to go, though. Make this last gesture . . .

The carriage was almost empty, and as always he examined the few shuttered faces and imagined the purposes behind them. London! Would he ever tire of its infinite variety? Of the unique, extraordinary way its whole ambience could change by the turning of a corner, a short vanishing underground? This South London concrete, really, was light-years away, not fifteen minutes, from Gower Street.

The blocks were identical, but he remembered which one without looking at the numbers. The graffiti-crazed lift was working, but as he came out of it he heard the baying of youths. The acoustics, though, of the long horizontal and vertical vistas of concrete made them seem nearer than they were; no one was to be seen on the balcony which stretched past this particular row of front doors.

Tate's was opened to him by one adolescent boy with a sulky face, who stood mutely suspicious. Tate's kid brother, smouldering in the background of so many press photographs.

"Is Frank in?"

"What if he is?"

"All right, Billy." Frank Tate had eased into the narrow hallway behind the boy. It was a day, thought Neil fleetingly, of narrow hallways.

"What d'you want?"

"I want your help."

He hadn't known the sort of reception he'd get from Frank Tate, but really, beside the look on the boy's face it was almost cordial. Well, it was noncommittal. Tate, though, was grown-up enough to know that Neil had had no alternative to arresting him . . .

"All right, Billy," said Tate again, and the boy lounged along the hallway and out through a door which gave a glimpse of another concrete balcony rail and another balcony opposite.

Tate, when Neil had first seen him, had looked more like the boy than he did now, although it was hard to say just where the change was.

"In here."

There was yellow paper on the walls, badly applied, the darker yellow of the flower pattern didn't match across the strips. But it was clean, like the cheap furniture, and the room was impersonally tidy. Tate sprawled onto a chair and Neil sat down on the sofa at right angles.

Tate was half smiling. "You want my help."

"Yes. I want to know if Juliet Payne—Marilyn—ever said anything to give you a clue. About herself, if not about who she was afraid of."

"She never said she was afraid of anyone. She never said anything about herself."

"Never?" It was an effort to continue casual.

"I told you. Look . . ." Tate leaned forward so that his face was quite close to Neil's. This time there was no smell of sweat. "That bird and I, we made it—right?—we had a few drinks and a few laughs and that was all."

It was strange, but he didn't resent Tate. By the time Tate was on the scene, Juliet's damage was done. "She didn't ever say why she was only going to be able to see you once a month?"

"Look." Tate flopped back in the chair. It wasn't a warm day, but he gave the impression of a man flaked out by heat. "When I saw her, I saw her because she came into that bar." The bar where they hadn't been able to tell the police anything either. Where, for him, all this had begun. "Or because she phoned me. She was a good kid but I wasn't waiting for her, for God's sake."

"That last time. You didn't think there was anything different about her?"

"Different? Do me a favour, I wasn't looking for anything different. And I didn't find it."

It was perhaps his realization of Juliet's nerve which chilled him most. That she had so perfectly played the part for which she had had no training. He got to his feet.

"No. Of course not. Thanks."

"Any time. I don't mean that, of course."

"Of course not. Good-bye, Frank. Good luck."

There was silence along the concrete now, except for his own footsteps. He had to wait for the lift, whipped by the artificial winds funnelled from all directions to the small confluence where he stood. The lift was empty, and there was no one outside it on the ground. He found himself unnaturally aware of his progress, a turn here, a second turn, silence still unless his own steps were sounding. Heedless sunshine dazzling down the narrow concrete path to the street. The last alcove. The first blow . . .

It felled him, so that he saw only a blur of legs. Three, four pairs, a shoe coming at him. Another.

As he passed out, through the mist a faint sense of relief . . .

He knew he hadn't been out long, perhaps only a minute, but the hostile feet had had time to run out of earshot. The one pair of feet beside him now were female and noncombatant, and instead of the hoarse cries of mutual encouragement there was a quiet woman's voice asking him if he was all right. Then a woman's face beside his, suddenly obliterating the well-shaped legs on which he had been refocusing his eyes.

"I think so." It hurt him to sit up, but he could do it. Stand up, too, if not quite upright.

"I'd better take you round the corner to the hospital. What happened?"

"I was jumped."

He hadn't actually seen Billy Tate, but he knew. Not that he would say. Except to Frank, on the telephone, to keep an eye out for his kid brother. Well, it was loyalty of a kind.

"Lost anything?"

The woman sounded businesslike, and was young and pretty as well.

As he expected, nothing had gone from his pockets. "You must have scared them off. Thank you."

"Thank you for drawing the fire." He saw she had been frightened. "My car's just outside. I heard feet but I didn't see anyone. How many?"

"I should think five or six. Young." He was walking quite well between the last few yards of concrete walls, although he was beginning to be aware of his chest and stomach. Probably sensible to look in at the hospital. "What are you doing here?"

"Paying a social call. An official one." On Frank Tate, perhaps? "What are *you* doing?"

Each knew that the other couldn't be on home ground. Till such assumptions could cease to be made, England would have a class system.

"I'm a policeman. I was following a hunch. Nothing to do with this outfit. I'd rather leave it at that."

"Of course, I wouldn't dream . . ."

She said she would wait for him, but he wanted her to go. He wanted the incident to disappear into the past as unobtrusively as possible.

"Thanks, I'll get a taxi." He could see she was disappointed, and was glad his awareness didn't interest him. The doctor who saw him was less prepared to mind his own business, but subsided when Neil took out his ID.

"I don't think anything's broken, Inspector Carter, you've just collected some bad bruises. Take it easy."

"I'm driving down to the New Forest this evening; my wife's there."

"That would be irresponsible. Find a taxi and go and lie up for tonight at least. Live in London?"

"Yes."

"Phone by the bed?"

"Yes."

"Ring your wife."

He'd crawled into the new, wide white bed before realizing the irony of his single occupation of it. All his dreams, and now it was just a place to rest in alone . . . As he stretched gingerly for the telephone, it occurred to him he had never been less well equipped for the delicate task of not arousing either fear or anger in a situation which invited both . . .

"Neil, where are you?"

"I'm at the flat. I'm in our bed. I was jumped by some youths and I've got bruises. Only bruises, don't worry. I'm here under protest because the doctor I saw to be on the safe side made me promise not to drive the car. I'm all right though. Cathy?"

"I'm here, Neil, I just . . . I should have come up with you, I know I should, and you could have dropped me off and I would have been at the flat waiting for you. Darling, are you really all right?"

"Really. A few bruises." The distracting amusement of Cathy taking the blame made him too honest too early. "Actually, darling, I went to see Frank Tate last thing before setting off back to you. I thought he might just be able to tell me something helpful, but he couldn't, and when I left him I was jumped by his kid brother and friends. 'There's one for Frank' sort of thing. I didn't really see them, so I shan't tell anyone but you that it was more than bad luck. Cathy? Are you there?"

"I'm here." The two cold, flat words were enough to tell him he had made a mistake. "It seems to have been rather good luck that you weren't killed or crippled. Good luck for us both."

"Cathy . . ."

"You haven't changed, have you, Neil? Well, you'd better get some rest, try to recover."

The tightness in his chest, the difficulty in breathing, had only just come on.

"I won't. I'll come down."

"Don't be silly. Don't make things worse. We'll talk in the morning."

"I want to talk now."

"I don't want to talk now." Her voice was very small and unanimated. This, then, was Cathy when she was angry. And she was angry with him.

"All right, darling. I'll ring you first thing in the morning. I'll be fit as a fiddle by then. I'll be able to—"

"You don't know what you'll be like in the morning. Make some tea and take aspirins."

"They gave me something. Cathy—"

"Good night, Neil."

She had meant it; she had hung up.

The uncurtained square of window was navy blue, with one star.

As a gesture to his unfamiliar wife, rather than to his own inclination, he got out of bed and went into the kitchen and made a pot of tea. He took it back to bed with the whisky bottle and a glass and propped himself up to drink tea and whisky alternately and examine his strange dual sensation of regret and relief. Regret that he had acted as if he still had only himself to consider. Relief that he had been enabled to pay off his debt to Juliet Payne. Debt? The few moments in that bar, when he had chatted up Marilyn, that had been his contribution, however unheeding, to the degradation of Juliet Payne, and then he had failed to answer her call for help. But now he had been punished . . . He would, of course, eventually have told Cathy why he had been mugged, if he hadn't blurted it out so foolishly on the telephone, but he would never tell her his own real reaction to the assault, of that second of satisfaction. Perhaps even, subconsciously, he had gone south of the river to look for trouble . . .

The doorbell rang two or three times before he could disentangle it from his dreams. He climbed out of bed groaning, not just for his aches and pains but at the thought of Miss Prince on his step, eager and apologetic. If she'd spotted him staggering in, why had she taken so long to call, it must be late . . .

It took another few minutes to find his winter dressing gown in the other bedroom, and then he had to put it on carefully. He held it together as he peered through the spy hole.

Not at a distorted Miss Prince.

He wrenched the door open. Cathy picked up the second suitcase before he could reach for it.

"I'm sorry I had to get you out of bed. I hadn't taken any keys."

"Those cases . . ."

"They balanced." Almost without him noticing it she had put him back into bed and plumped his pillows, and was now giving him the pleasure of watching her dart about the room. "There was a train at a quarter past eight from Brockenhurst and I got a taxi. I've left the third case with the manager, we can go down for it any time."

"And I shan't have to spend my first night in our bed alone. I have changed, Cathy, I really—"

"I know."

"Thank you for coming home."

And now, too, Juliet had let him go. He knew now that she wouldn't haunt him, hadn't taken up residence at the back of his mind. Even the fact that he hadn't got anywhere with the investigation couldn't disturb him any more. At least, only in the usual way of its possible effect on his career and his relations with the chief and his sense of personal achievement.

The new experience of a platonic night and a totally uneventful day, being waited on by Cathy and doing a jigsaw puzzle seemed to set him so safely beyond recent events he felt strong enough by Sunday bedtime to start thinking aloud again about the case he was still on.

"The chief gave me the option of leaving the Bellfield end of things. That's what I'll do, I don't want to go back." He looked a question, and she nodded and smiled. "Although I don't know what else there is to do now in London, except haunt that club, and I think that's more a job for David. I can't think of any other way I can make another idiot of myself." Thank heaven the quarrel hadn't left any area they would have to avoid. "Oh, darling, I'm starting to think it must simply have been another of Juliet's clients who killed her. She was probably just making mischief by telephoning me, she was probably only expressing a general annoyance at having to go back to the forest as Miss Juliet Payne." It could be that he was testing himself, to see how total his recovery was. If so, it was holding up. He went deliberately on. "I haven't got anywhere, have I? I haven't eliminated anyone. Even Bertha Hazell could have made herself appear innocent by trying to appear clumsily guilty—when she really is guilty. Agatha Christie wrote a mystery story on those lines, and Bertha said once that she likes crime stories. No, I don't really believe that. But it's possible. And we still can't say that Mary Booth *didn't* do it. Nobody seems to have seen her or her sister during those fateful hours. We don't know whether Cowley's guilty or not . . ." A pang took him unawares. The thought that if he had let that letter lie in the Wendy house, an innocent Peter Cowley's life might still have been worth living. "I've done so much more harm than good on this one."

"That's nonsense. You're just feeling a bit sorry for yourself because of what's happened." That was probably true. "You've worked hard and conscientiously and unselfishly on this case." The prick of conscience, now, was so faint as to be negligible. Billy Tate and his gang had been a small price to pay. "If Peter Cowley is innocent, then he's a casualty, but people forget. And Bertha will always be his champion. I should think she must have broken that gold chain of hers by now. Did it survive the trick you played on her in the Hardman flat?"

"Yes. Yes, it did. I remember seeing it. And she didn't touch it, she didn't touch it at all. Cathy . . . That night in her house, when we went round to tell her Tate was in the clear and she made her confession . . . Did she touch it then?"

"D'you know . . . Now you mention it, she didn't. I remember that when we first went in I was looking out for her to start pulling at it, and noticing that she didn't. And then forgetting, when she dropped her bombshell. But I have this memory of her pulling, tugging at the chain . . ."

"It was the first time we went into her house. When we were sitting round in her parlour, she never let it alone. Cathy . . ." He sat up; if he could have done it, he would have bounded about the room. "I know now what it was that struck me about Bertha. First I gave her the chance to say she'd done the murder. Then I gave her the chance to say she'd been trying to protect Cowley—well, it was David who did that, actually, but it could as well have been me. Each time, she looked as if she couldn't believe her luck. That was why the one occasion reminded me of the other, not because she seemed both times to be looking through me. It was because I'd handed her a lifeline. I'll have to stop putting words into suspects' mouths."

"Neil, for once I'm not with you."

"The gold chain, darling, the gold chain."

It was easier to get the chief's telephone permission to take David on an ostensibly formal visit the next morning, than Cathy's to leave the flat. She agreed only when he'd promised to take a taxi to the office and then put David in the driving seat. In view of his aches and pains, she took less persuading to allow him a sleeping pill, which he wanted, really, to contract the time of waiting.

CHAPTER 15

He found John Hazell's number in the telephone book and rang it before leaving home. There was no reply.

That seemed strange at eight o'clock on a Monday morning, but the man could as well be away for the weekend or on holiday as making an early start at the office. The thought of perhaps not being able to contact him that day, that week, filled Neil with a furious impatience, uncomfortably fuelled as he waited for a taxi and then was driven in fits and starts through the choked streets. David was just outside the office talking to a fellow sergeant, and Neil whirled him inside and closed the door.

"I wasn't expecting you, governor. Not even your usual cool self."

"David, I think I see the light on Juliet Payne."

He left it at that; as yet, there was so much more of instinct than of reason. In the intervals of ringing Hazell's office and flat, he told David he'd fallen against the corner of a table, because David would notice that he had a tendency to wince. Also because David was going to be asked to drive. He endured David's facetious comments in uncompanionable silence. It was nine-fifteen when Hazell's office answered. David had made the call, and handed the receiver over.

"Is Mr. Hazell there?"

"I am afraid not." It was an unnaturally refined female voice. "To whom am I speaking?"

"It's a private call. Is he away? Are you expecting him?"

"I am expecting him, he is not away. As a matter of fact, he's usually here by now."

At ten o'clock Hazell had still not arrived at his office and there was still no reply from the flat. Neil went to see the chief and was uncharacteristically impassioned enough to get an extension of his brief.

"Come along, Sergeant."

The grey April sky seemed to suit the dark red mansion flats off Kensington High Street. Hazell's was on the first floor, up a mottled marble staircase. Neil and David could hear the bell shrill through the heavy door, but nobody answered it. There was no answer, either, from the identical door opposite.

"Someone who *has* gone to work," said Neil. "Here goes, then."

With the mortice lock, it took about ten minutes.

Inside, everything seemed to be too tall for its breadth. At first he thought there must be curtains drawn, it was so dark, but that was because of the paintwork and heavy furniture, and the fact that the sitting-room window was the only one not facing onto a wall. The video camera on its tripod was an incongruity in the sitting room, quite apart from the neatly written note attached to it telling the police that the cassette was in the video machine and ready for playing. Sitting room, high thin dining room, two bedrooms, were immaculate, and as impersonal as Hazell himself. The kitchen was very different from Bertha Hazell's cottage kitchen, but reminded Neil of it because of being so clinically clean and tidy. John Hazell must have washed up the lunch that Sunday Neil and Cathy had called on Bertha . . .

He opened the closed door with the glass panels last, it was so obviously the bathroom. It was tiled all over in white, the only really light place in the flat, which was probably why the impact was so horrible. Hazell was in there, on the floor, slumped against the bath. This time Neil didn't have to be close to pick up his individual smell—the smell of a butcher's shop, because most of Hazell's blood seemed to be splashed around the white tiles beside him and on the white side of the bath and the white floor.

The putty-coloured face had taken on a yellow tinge, but the eyelids were flickering. The wrists had been partly tourniqueted by being wedged between the knees and sticking against one another when the legs fell apart. But the pulse was very low.

"Help me, David."

They bound the wrists as tightly as their strength would let them. Hazell's eyes opened once or twice, but the eyeballs were rolled up. It was difficult not to slip over in the blood, and several times Neil saved himself with savage penalties to his ribs and stomach. Hazell was wearing only an elegant silk dressing gown. He had set his scene.

When David had telephoned, he brought cushions and they transferred Hazell's head to them. Then Neil carefully washed himself space and got down beside Hazell and talked encouragingly to him until the ambulance arrived. Hazell said, "Just as well, just as well," a couple of times. He didn't seem to be rebelling against what he had done, but Neil supposed one would reach a stage where one wouldn't or couldn't. Just before there were voices in the hall, Hazell said urgently, "In the sitting room. All set up. I'm sorry." He didn't say any more, although his eyelids were still moving when they took him away. They'd start the transfusions in the ambulance.

The video machine was on top of the television set. He might have had a sneak preview of the film Hazell had made, but although he'd closed the bathroom door he felt he was carrying the fresh butcher's smell with him, and he had to go back in there. After he'd been sick he still felt it, but it didn't bother him so much. He washed his hands and his shoes, and as he came back into the hall the doorbell rang again.

The superintendent walked in first. The super was the only man Neil knew who made the chief look small. Physically. The super was very tall as well as broad and moved as if he was perpetually taking part in a royal procession. Once, and unknown to either of the senior men, Neil had seen him make the chief look psychologically small as well, but generally they each knew and played their complementary roles. Neil was rather glad the super had come. Not just because he wouldn't be able to forget, now, Carter's key role in the Juliet Payne affair. Also because the super was inclined to think well of him already and the chief would have to be a bit more polite.

David had brought upright chairs in from the dining room, turning the sitting room into a private cinema. The word "nasties" kept coming into Neil's mind. And there was a chance it wasn't entirely irrelevant.

He activated the video and sat down as the fourth in the front and only row. The film opened at once upon John Hazell, sitting in his dark office suit in the room where they were watching him, against the wall where the ebony African mask hung, so that it leered at them in double image. He was behind his desk, his hands loosely holding the video control.

"When you see this," said the video of John Hazell expressionlessly, "I shall be dead."

He could be right. It didn't seem to matter. All that mattered was that he should tell them more than the fact that he had killed Juliet Payne.

"If that foolish woman Bertha Hazell hadn't attempted to protect me, Peter Cowley wouldn't now be under suspicion of the murder of Juliet Payne, and the police wouldn't be ready to turn their attention on me as the other man within her orbit."

Would they have become ready if he hadn't remembered the gold chain (if Cathy hadn't reminded him) and two similar reactions by Bertha Hazell?

"Not that I'm particularly concerned for Cowley, or about whether the police move on to me. I've simply had enough of it all. I don't want to carry on with the memory of it. The memory's not to be lived with. But Bertha is a fool." There was hardly more expression in Hazell's voice than in his face. The chief grunted, the super crossed his legs the other way. "She hasn't said anything since that time she came to the flat and I told her no, but she hasn't given up. I thought if I could get to like Juliet, or pretend to like her, flaunt her under Bertha's nose, her aunt's nose, she might stop hoping. Bertha's hopes have tentacles which stretch from Bellfield to Kensington. Even when my father was alive, I was uneasy . . ."

Neil saw the hands tighten together as, with a subdued click, the picture very slightly altered. Hazell had broken off there, resumed.

"If Bertha hadn't telephoned me that Saturday night, I wouldn't have told her I was taking Juliet out to lunch the next day and she would never have suspected me. That was part of her presumption, suspecting me when I'd told her I had nothing to do with it."

Bertha should see this, she really should. So far at least.

Even on the video, he could tell Hazell's muscles were tautening.

"It must have been a couple of years since I'd seen Juliet, I'd kept away from Bellfield because of Bertha. I calculated she was sixteen but apparently she wasn't, she was fifteen." Had the lower lip trembled? "I looked up Hardman in the book, as Bertha suggested, and rang about seven o'clock on the Saturday evening. Juliet answered. I didn't particularly remember her voice, and anyway it wasn't childish any more. She seemed surprised, then suddenly enthusiastic. She asked me to go round to the flat at twelve noon next day."

The hands tightened again, but the picture didn't break. It was good enough to show the knuckles whitening.

"I got there on time and went up in the lift and walked along the way she'd told me. I rang the bell and the door was opened by — by a woman, I thought, who stood there looking at me." Neil could see the shine coming on Hazell's forehead and top lip. The hands had separated, and the empty one was straining at the desk top. "I know of course with hindsight that she expected me to recognize her. I didn't. When she smiled I think it was because she realized how much richer her revenge was going to be than she'd dreamed."

Revenge? Neil's fingertips were at it again, severally tingling. He spread them on his lap.

"She asked me to come in, she told me Juliet had had to go out unexpectedly. She said she was Marilyn something, I've forgotten the other name she used, a friend of the Hardmans, and she hoped I would let her entertain me until Juliet got back. She wouldn't be back for an hour. Nobody would."

Hazell put his hand up to his tie, brought it down again without touching or loosening it. Remembering even now, Neil thought, his image.

"She gave me a drink. She flirted with me. I thought she was in her twenties. I thought"—briefly Hazell bowed his head, as if at an admission of weakness—"she was attractive. She gave me another drink. She made me feel"—he bowed his head again—"she found me attractive too. She took me into a bedroom to show me a picture on the wall. She told me there was still half an hour before anyone would arrive. Juliet or anyone. She laughed when she said that. She—" The hands were together again. "She was on the bed, she held her hand out, laughing. I thought: It's nothing to *her* . . ." For a few seconds John Hazell closed his eyes, then shot them wide open. Too much to look at, inside. His face was still expressionless. "We lay for a few moments—afterwards— then she sat up and looked at me and said . . ." The face turned aside, as if the camera in front of it was a memory. "She said, 'I'm Juliet, what have you done, John?' Then somehow she altered her face and her manner and I saw it, I knew . . ."

The machine clicked. Only the second time. But even Hazell would have needed a break at that point.

"It was a terrible thing, that it was so easy." He had wiped his face. "Strangling her was only pinching myself to wake up from a bad dream."

For a second, dreadfully, the face contorted, blurred. Then resumed its smooth definition. Someone jerked in his chair; Neil thought it was the super.

"But I hadn't wakened up. I wiped the door handle with my handkerchief, and the other doors where I'd gone through, and the glasses, I washed up the one I'd used and put it away. Then I went downstairs—I didn't use the lift—and out of the building and into my car and away. It was ten to one and I didn't see anyone. But I had to get in touch with Bertha, because of her knowing I'd arranged to take Juliet out for lunch. And because of that, I had to tell her what had happened. I rang her as soon as I got home, and I said that I'd arrived at the flat door and found it open and gone in and found Juliet dead. I told her I couldn't have done anything and that there was no point in getting involved, it wouldn't do any of us any good, or my business, and that I'd left without being seen. It was difficult, keeping that silly bitch from going to pieces by telephone, it would have been easier if I'd seen her, but I couldn't risk that. I was less impatient with her than I usually am and I got her to promise to make sure she received the news as if it really was news and not to tell the police about my inviting Juliet to lunch. I told her I'd come and stay with her for the funeral and we could talk then. She hung on to that."

Why did people give themselves so much less than they deserved?

"I thought when I came to Bellfield she'd blackmail me into sleeping with her, but she didn't, I did her an injustice.

"Oh yes, I must tell you what she couldn't tell you when she made her ridiculous confession. The bedside clock was knocked off onto the floor and the glass broke. It must have been stopped about twelve-forty."

For the first time, Hazell leaned back in his chair. "That's all, really. And it's too much. Too much to bear. I'm sorry. I'm very sorry."

There was another click, a blank screen, and for Neil a suffocating sense of disappointment, opportunity lost. He hadn't realized how much more he had hoped for from John Hazell. First in the flesh. And then from the screen. The man might be alive still, but Neil's hope had died.

Revenge?

He was putting out his hand to the switch, the chief's chair was creaking, as John Hazell reappeared on the screen before them wearing the dressing gown in which he had been taken away.

"Sit down, Neil," said the chief irritably.

"Yes, governor."

"I don't think it's because I want to live a few moments longer," said John Hazell. "I think it's because I owe it to Juliet to explain her. I'm the only one who knows."

Neil could hardly sit still. He noticed that it wasn't just the dressing gown that was different, it was the whole bearing of the man, the relaxation of each feature, the loosely lying hands, even the piece of hair which had fallen forward. Shriven? But it shouldn't be so easy.

"Nothing can do me any good." Resignation, more likely. "But I want to tell the truth about Juliet, why she was doing what made me kill her. When I'm dead there'll be nobody left to tell it. I hesitate only because Bertha must never know, and Bertha one way or another will get to see this video. However Bertha has plagued me, I would never wish that truth upon her. It would be double murder. I ask for your entire discretion."

Oh yes, you will have it, don't hesitate, tell me.

"Everyone thought Bertha, my father, and Juliet were a happy little family. Perhaps they were, until one day when Juliet was twelve. I was staying at the cottage, in those days I quite often stayed there at weekends. Bertha was out somewhere, Juliet was up in the little bedroom which was kept for her, my father was pottering about. I was mowing the lawn, and over the noise of the mower I heard Juliet scream. I didn't give her time to scream when I killed her, I remembered those screams. I ran upstairs and into the little bedroom. Juliet was sprawled on the bed half naked with her legs spread out. When she saw me, she screamed again and tried to crawl down by the wall. I covered her up and sat by the bed talking to her until she was quiet. Then I went downstairs. My father was slumped in a chair in the sitting room. He said in a tired, defeated sort of way, 'I'm sorry, John.' He had a conviction for interfering with a schoolgirl, I think it was what killed my mother. I hadn't been old enough to help him out of that one, I only knew about it because I found the cutting, just before he married Bertha. He had convinced me the urge had gone, perhaps he convinced himself.

"I took Juliet back to Bellfield House. I told her her uncle wasn't well, I told Henry Juliet wasn't well. I didn't know what Juliet was going to do, or say, but I acted as if she wasn't going to do or say anything. I was already uneasy about Bertha, but I wanted to spare her and I wanted to help my father although I despised him. I despise most people, really, I always have. Or perhaps it dates from when I first learned about my father. The irony is that from that moment the one person I didn't despise was Juliet; I thought that perhaps one day . . . Of course it wasn't just to get Bertha off my back that I asked Juliet to lunch. I wanted to see her again." The click came as the face contorted. When John Hazell reappeared, his eyes and nose were faintly pink. The irony could have been doing that to Neil's features too. "Juliet didn't do anything or say anything. Except, of course, that she didn't run in and out of Ivy Cottage any more, she only went when Bertha invited her, and I'm sure she was never alone with my father again. And of course he cooperated, he made sure he was never again alone with her. He died within three months. Of a heart attack, but I think it was brought on because of how much

he disliked himself. As I dislike myself now, perhaps. Between us
we did quite a job, didn't we, Dad and I? But I don't think Juliet
had a chance, and my part in it might just have been merciful."

The super and the chief got to their feet as David switched the
machine off.

"All right, Neil," said the chief.

"Well done, Carter," said the super.

They were all avoiding one another's eyes, and the two senior
men made directly for the door.

"Pack it up and bring it with you," said the chief. "Better ring
for the team to go over the place and make sure there isn't anything else."

"Yes, governor."

He sat down again on his dining chair, wanting Cathy with
him. David left him alone for a few minutes, then came back and
took the cassette out and said the team was on its way. The doorbell rang.

"It can't be them yet, Neil, unless they're clairvoyant. I'll go."

He wondered if he was clairvoyant himself. As soon as he saw
Bertha Hazell in the last of the narrow hallways, he realized he
had known she would come.

"Mr. Carter . . ."

"Come in, Bertha, come in here." Unconsciously he had reverted to their earlier relationship. He steered her past the sitting
room, into the dining room. John Hazell's message had of course
been removed, but if the video camera had been brought in for the
occasion and didn't represent one of his hobbies, she would want
to know why it was there.

"Sit down, Bertha." There were still two easy chairs in the
room, but she remained standing, looking round her as if Hazell
might have concealed himself behind one of the slabs of furniture.

"Where's John? He didn't answer the telephone, and I couldn't
wait, I had to see him. Where is he?" She saw Neil properly for
the first time. "What are you doing here, Mr. Carter? Oh, please
. . ."

She clutched his arm and he helped her to one of the chairs, his
ribs groaning.

"John's dead, Bertha. He took his life. I think you know why."

The lie was better than her pursuing Hazell to hospital, maybe hearing an unconscious replay of his final revelation. Anyway, by now it could be the truth.

He caught her as she swayed forward. He found her brandy for the second time and sat down on the floor beside her chair, hoping she wouldn't get round yet to asking him how it had been done. Eventually she said, staring at the vase of dried leaves inside the huge mahogany surround of the fireplace, "I think I knew, really, right away, when he told me he'd been there. Then, when I learned what she did in that flat, and he shouted in his sleep . . ." She looked imploringly at Neil. "I *did* kill her, really, you see, I sent John to her. What she'd become . . . Perhaps we can't blame John . . ." If Hazell died, it really would be a good thing for her to see most of the video. The part before he changed into his dressing gown. There wouldn't be much of an editing job, it would just have to end where Hazell had originally intended it to end. And they would have to cut out the reference to revenge. Before she saw it, he'd go through it himself, to make sure they'd got it right . . .

She was rummaging in her bag, holding up two keys. "If you hadn't answered the door. I'd have let myself in. When John was ill once at Ivy Cottage, just before Leonard died, I looked for his flat keys, and I found them, and I had other ones cut. Before Leonard died." The truth, the whole, the unnecessary, the shocking truth, was on Bertha too. "I came here once, twice, in the afternoon when I knew John was at work, and I got into his bed." She glared at Neil.

If you hadn't answered the door, I'd have let myself in.

If he hadn't suddenly understood, hadn't come at once this Monday morning, Bertha would have discovered John Hazell. Infinitely more terrible, she would have discovered and played the whole cassette. He might not have done anything for the dead, but he'd done something for the living.

There was one more thing he wanted to ask her.

"Bertha. Even though I didn't believe your confession, I wondered about what you said happened to make you snap. When you said Juliet taunted you, made you feel old and stupid. Forgive me, but that part of it had a ring of truth."

"It was true." He thought he was seeing her, in a flash, as she would look in ten or fifteen years' time. "When I took her to the station that last time, I said I wished she wasn't so secretive and she turned on me. I drove off and wept. I never saw her again."

"Come away now," he said gently. "We'll take you home."

He told David to stay behind, but the team was on the stairs. Just as well, he wasn't supposed to be driving. David said he was going to take Neil home, then drive Bertha back to Bellfield. He was glad to say yes, thank you. They were safely clear of the building when Bertha asked what John had done, and where. He couldn't protect her imagination, but she didn't show any fresh reaction, she was already surfeited.

He rang the doorbell instead of getting out his key. He heard Cathy's running step, as he had heard it so often when he had crossed the landing for sympathy and coffee.

"I'll lie down," he said, "while I tell you."

She sat in the armchair in the corner, and didn't speak until he had finished.

"How did you know, Neil? What were you saying to me about Bertha's gold chain?"

"You reminded me; if you hadn't reminded me I mightn't have realized . . . You saw her twice under particular stress, I saw her three times. She only pulled at that chain when Hazell was there. You made me think—why? Then I remembered the sort of incredulous look on her face, first when I'd suggested she could have killed Juliet, then when David suggested she'd made her confession to protect Cowley. The same look each time. As I said to you last night—as if she couldn't believe her luck. And all she had to say about worrying whether Juliet had provoked Cowley—for Cowley read Hazell. Poor Bertha. Grief and jealousy all tied up together.

"One more thing—which I can only ever say to you: I suddenly felt satisfied." He stretched his arms and legs, and the pain was less. "I think Juliet presented herself to John Hazell as Marilyn because she wanted to shock him, even to seduce him—after all, she had a score to settle with the Hazell family—but as Hazell said himself, she hadn't reckoned on *deceiving* him. It must have been a glorious bonus when she realized he didn't know her. But

POS2

at the same time, before he arrived she was frightened of what she was going to do if I didn't go to the flat and prevent her. She might even have been planning to blackmail him for being with an underage girl. Certainly, if she wanted her double life to continue, she must have intended to keep him quiet that way. But whatever she had in mind, I know now the person Juliet was frightened of was herself." What else had John Hazell said? *Juliet didn't do anything or say anything.* "Oh, darling. That awful, lonely, grown-up courage. No wonder she changed."

Cathy got up from the armchair and came and lay on the bed beside him. "This is awfully decadent, but I'll get us some lunch in a moment. I wish she hadn't been so brave."

"So do I." Juliet might not be going to haunt him, but there would always be a place too tender to touch. What had Bertha said? *She died in her sins.*

He wasn't sure about his own God, but Cathy's was a God of mercy . . .

"Perhaps John Hazell wasn't always so impersonal, Neil. Perhaps he changed too. All his energies going into just bearing it."

"Perhaps." The telephone rang. It was the chief, considerately to tell him Hazell was dead.

When he had replaced the receiver, Cathy carefully put her arms round him. "I'm glad your mother didn't really come from the forest. I couldn't ever feel welcome there again."

They must snap out of it. "Some corner of England forever a foreign field? I know what you mean. But it won't always feel like that."

"I liked Bellfield. I liked Bertha. We abused her hospitality however you look at it. It won't do any good, but in a little while, when she's seen that cassette and got used to it, I'm going to write to her."

Bertha wrote back, talking about summer in her garden and along the lanes. She said she was a free woman again, and asked them to go and stay.

ABOUT THE AUTHOR

Eileen Dewhurst was born in Liverpool and educated there at Huyton College, and later at Oxford. As a free-lance journalist, she has published many articles in the Liverpool *Daily Post,* the *Illustrated Liverpool News, Punch,* and *The Times.* She has written plays that have been performed in England and is the author of seven previous crime novels, including *The House That Jack Built, Whoever I Am,* and *Curtain Fall.*